HIDDEN TREASURES

John Harrington Burns
Copyright © 2000

HIDDEN TREASURES

By
John Harrington Burns © 2001

ISBN 1-59146-081-6

Cover Photo by Nancy Bernhard
Cover by Mary Kay Davis

First Edition: published June 6, 2001, by Charm Write Publishing, 2448 E. 39th St., Anderson, IN 46013, USA.

Special Edition: edited and published by GrannyDragon.com, c/o Mary Kay Davis, 2209 Hamilton Lane, Grants Pass, OR 97527, USA, November 27, 2001, grannydragon@grannydragon.com, http://www.grannydragon.com

Second Edition: published by Crystal Dreams Publications PO Box 698, Dover, TN 37058, USA.
January 2002,
ISBN 1-59146-081-6

http://www.crystaldreamspub.com

crystaldreamspub.com
P.O. Box 698   Dover, TN 37058

DEDICATION

Dedicated to Mary, who dedicated her life to me.

INDEX

Beyond half-closed doors are
Hidden Treasures.

Come follow me through a half-closed door,
That leads to a passageway beyond this realm.
In that furtive corridor your fantasy will soar.
You'll commandeer the imaginary helm
To embrace arcane, incredible pleasures,
For beyond a half-closed door are Hidden Treasures.

Sla'n-agat,

John Harrington Burns

SYLLABIC BYWAYS

Sometimes I wish
   That I could climb
      Inside a book and live
         Between the pages.

I'd wander through
   The sentences
      Of lofty thoughts
         By well respected sages.

I'd be a friend
   To brand new words
      And get to know their
         Origins and ages.

I'd scale the Alps
   Of abstract prose
      And measure poems'
         Iambic feet by stages.

The title page
   Will send me off,
      'Bon Voyage, enjoy your trip,'
         With apostrophes and colons.

I'd pause beside a comma
   To understand their clauses.
      I'd soar among the slopes
         And ride the crest of predicates.

Then descend the valleys
  Of subjunctive moods
    Though they may be brooding.

Oh, to live and laugh with adjectives,
  Gerunds, nouns and verbs subjective.
    I'd even dangle with participles
      Who found me quite impressible.

I'd split a few infinitives
  In spite of their derivatives.
    I'd party with past and present tenses
      Perhaps I'd even lose my senses.

I'd become a friend and mentor
  To a neglected neutered gender.
    I'd race through every chapter
      Filled with euphoric rapture.

Don't you sometimes wish
  That you could climb inside a book
    And live between the pages?

*** *** ***

THE MONDAY NIGHT GAME

He swung around and sarcastically said, "You know, you're no help." Then he turned back to the refrigerator and continued to move bottles and containers around as he continued speaking.

"I'm searching for the leftover chicken. Do you think you could give me a helping hand?"

She stared him down. Never uttering a sound.

He was caught between the glare in her eyes and the light from the refrigerator. Both were cold and icy.

"I can't find the damned chicken. I know it's in there. I put it away myself last night."

He took out the butter dish and placed it on the counter.

"I can't count on you to help."

She adored him, but she didn't move.

He delved into the refrigerator again.

"Here's that freaking chicken leg, hiding behind the Bud. Now, if I was smart, I woulda taken that out first. But no. I was thinking of you and getting supper out."

He put the chicken down near the butter and turned to her.

"I'm gonna open this bottle before I do anything else, so you'll just have to wait if you have anything planned."

He opened his beer and rested against the counter, taking a long swallow. "Where the hell is the bread now?" All I want is chicken, bread, beer and football. It's Monday night, isn't it? Say something. Let me know I'm welcomed home at least."

She ignored his tantrum. She loved him no matter what his mood or disposition. She'd wait until he calmed down. Then she'd make her move.

"Typical female. I go out and work my ass off, for what? I come home and gotta make my own supper." He put the beer to his lips and chug-a-lugged it all the way down, then threw the empty into the wastebasket.

She heard a similar story every night. She turned her head. She knew more was coming no matter what she attempted to do. She could not stop him. It was like a ritual with him. She practiced patience, while he burned.

"My old lady was right. She predicted it would end up like this."

Now it's the 'old lady' story. She just listened and kept silent. *Let him get it out of his system.*

"I don't know why I live with you. Where the hell is a clean butter knife? See, I can yell and still no response from you. Damn dummy!"

He reached under the counter for the silverware drawer and gave it a yank. He applied a little too much power in his pull. Silverware splattered all over the kitchen floor.

"It's your fault this happened. If you showed a little appreciation that I'm home, this wouldn't have happened. But don't move. Don't touch a thing. Like always, I get to pick up the pieces. You just stay where you are."

She had no intentions of moving. *He did it. Serves him right.*

"On second thought, why should I pick it up now? It's going to be a long night. I think I'll go down to the corner and get a six pack. Wanna take a walk?"

In spite of it all, he really did love her. He just proved it. She rose and rushed into his arms.

He reached for her leash.

***

BLEEDING HEARTS AND LADY'S-SLIPPERS

On a lazy summer's day designed for meditation and lemonade, Henry Compton sat on his porch, dozing in his wheelchair. Occasionally, his jaw dropped to his chest as his head bobbed and nodded in and out of forty winks. A fly tickled his nose and wheedled him out of his slumber. He blinked a couple of times, then stretched his eyebrows to exorcise the sleepiness from his eyes. Slowly, he opened them wide, only to gaze at the Wisteria vines towering along the porch's railing to the porch roof. Their roots went deep into his memory. The old fear that the vines would reach out and wrap around his body overwhelmed him. He sensed an impending embrace of death. His fingers trembled, and his clammy hands lost their grip on the wheels of his chair.

Impotent and withered, he bowed his head and succumbed to the terror of the vines enshrouding his mausoleum. He took a deep, hard breath and sucked the air as far into his lungs as his frail body would allow. If only he had the strength, he'd rise up, out of his confinement, pull those vines up from their roots, and hurl them to Kingdom Come. Maybe then his nights would descend gently and tranquil.

On the other side of the vines, the sun moved from its apex and dropped behind a cloud.

His weak, drained body was cold and damp with the sweat of fear. He leaned back and exhaled a sigh.

From some dark, murky room an antique clock chimed half past noon. The delicate intonation of time passing triggered Henry's heart to skip a beat, then quicken its rhythm. The clamor of his sister bustling around inside the house brought him into reality.

"Delphinia! What in the hell are you doing in there?" The screen door squeaked open and Delphinia came through, carrying a luncheon tray. Her trim, neat appearance disguised the dominant strength that lay hidden beneath her neatly pressed cotton print. Her sweetness and femininity, like the lovely smell of lilac water on her delicate skin, was applied only for effect. For all her advanced years, Delphinia had the enthusiasm and energy of a woman much younger. She paused and waited until she heard the screen door slam shut behind her before crossing the porch to her brother.

"Here's your lunch, Henry." She set the tray down on his lap. "I fixed up some delicious chicken soup and a nice sandwich. I made it from the ham that was left over from last night. I put in a crisp leaf of lettuce and a dab of mayo. Just the way you like it. And look, I even added a vase with a lovely red rose. All for you."

"Well, isn't that just ducky," Henry mocked. "Why the hell are you setting it down on my lap? Want me to spill hot soup all over myself? Ain't I got enough pain and troubles as it is? I swear, Delphie, you act queerer as the days go by."

"I see you're in one of your more pleasant moods today, brother dear." Delphinia took the tray away from Henry and put it in the middle of the table beside his wheelchair. "Don't you ever have a smile for me?"

"Cut that phony sweetness out. I don't want your stinking rose."

"Why not? It's a perfectly beautiful rose. Why do you have to be so ornery all the time? Besides, I cut it from the rose bush in the back yard. I thought you'd appreciate it."

"Well, I don't. Because with you, there's always an ulterior meaning behind everything you do. For all I know, one of these delicious meals you concoct just for me might contain one of your special ingredients. Maybe this here soup could be laced with rat poison, and I could fall over dead before I get to swallow one spoonful."

"Oh, not again."

"I wouldn't put it past you. Get this damned rose the hell away from me. It smells like a wake."

"And you say I say queer things. You're the queer one, Henry dear. However, when you go to your next wake, you won't be able to smell the flowers."

"And just what is that supposed to mean?"

"Whatever you want it to. Delphinia stood tall and erect over the frail, bony-framed Henry. "After all these years, you continue to say the same thing every time I put a meal in front of you. When are you going to get it through you head that I will never use any kind of poison, because poison would cast suspicion on me. I couldn't have that, could I, my dear brother?"

"No. Suspicion has never fallen on you." A sardonic smile curled Henry's lips. His feeble appearance belied his following Delphinia into this world by six years.

"Oh, dear brother, how many times must I remind you that we both promised Mother to look after each other. In all sincerity, I intend to look after you right up until your very last breath. I will see that when you die, there will be no shadow of suspicion. You can trust me on that. I'll admit looking after you has filled my days, but these last few months have taken their toll on me. I'm getting weary. Our time together is growing short, brother. When I kill you, it won't be by poison."

"How nice you said that. Like you had it rehearsed. But I know you too well. You're a good one to talk about sincerity after all your lies, not to mention the damage you've done."

Delphinia pretended she didn't hear what her brother had said. She circled around back of him. She leaned over and pushed the hair away from his forehead. She spoke softly, almost whispering.

"I've notice you're starting to grow those wispy old hairs on your ear lobes. That's a sign that senility is approaching."

Henry leaned back and let Delphinia run her fingers through his hair. In a rare moment of outwardly displayed sibling affection, Henry lent himself willingly to his sister's touch. She caressed his head in a gentle manner and held his face up to hers. He raised his eyes and met his sister's gaze.

"Remind me to trim them and the hairs in your nose later this afternoon."

Delphinia pushed Henry's head away and giggled. Henry grabbed his sister's wrists and pulled her around to his side.

"You're crazier than I thought if you think I'm going to let you near me with a pair of scissors." Henry released his grip. "It'll never happen. You know damn well Ernie, the barber, is coming over after church on Sunday. He'll take care of the hairs you're so worried about. I'd never let you near me with any kind of a sharp instrument. Now stand back away from me, where I can see you without looking up."

Delphinia smelled his fear. She rubbed her wrists. Although her brother's grip was powerless, his gnarled hands easily bruised her skin.

"Hush up, you old fool. Doctor Boland will be here soon to give you a check up. Do you want him to see us going at each other?"

"Afraid he'd see you as you really are? Anyway, why in the hell is he coming to see me. I didn't call him. I don't need him."

"I don't know why he wants to see you. Maybe he's got some bad news he wants to tell you. Hurry up and finish your lunch so I can clean up your mess."

Henry put a spoon of soup to his lips. "Soup's not hot enough."

"If you don't finish every drop of that soup, I'll take it in the house and heat it boiling hot, then come out and spill it all over your lap."

Henry, in an exaggerated gesture, placed the spoon back on the tray. He stretched his lips and grimaced vindictively at his sister. "Watch and see what I think of you and your god damned cold soup." Henry picked up the tray and dropped it to the floor.

"Well, that's vengeful. Soup's all over everything. Now Doctor Boland will surely see how far you've regressed. You can't even hold onto a tray. It can stay there for all I care." Delphinia shrugged and retreated.

"Delphinia you can sop that up and go heat it as hot as you want."

Delphinia put her hands on her hips and closed her eyes. "Henry," she smirked as she nodded her head from side to side, "you'll never know what a favor you've done for me." Delphinia stepped around Henry's slop and walked to the side of the porch. She picked up the Agatha Christie book she kept open on the table and sat on an age-old, weather-beaten green wicker settee that had been fashionable during the presidency of Franklin D. Roosevelt. She skimmed through a page or two. Deciding not to read, she put the book down and gazed out, peering through the vines.

"You know, the Wisteria vines growing up in front of the porch keep the neighbors from actually seeing what we are doing here, yet we can look out between these old vines and blossoms and get a pretty good view of what's going on in the neighborhood. Those vines sure are strong and thick. Aren't they? I remember when Daddy brought them home. They were so small. Who would've thought they would get so tall and live so long."

"I bet you do remember," Henry snapped. "In fact, I know you remember quite clearly."

"Henry, you're tiptoeing through quicksand. If you're going to dig things up, I will too. You did your little contributing also. You went out and got those Bleeding Hearts and Lady's Slippers."

"You told me that we needed something to cover the ground better. I remember. And I'll never forget what you made me do."

"I can remember little pleasantries as well, you know, like Dorothea and Dandy. They were such lovely little girls."

"You old bitch, don't bring that up! I'm going to kill you yet. I wish I could get up and leave you and this god damned place forever."

"You had your chances but you were too greedy. I just love that part in Momma's will that says the first one to move out forfeits his half of the ownership of this house to the survivor. Notice, I said 'his.'" Delphinia smiled. "You stayed on. Face it, dear brother, you're going to die here on this Wisteria covered front porch. And I'm going to be the one to bury you."

"That'll be the day," Henry sneered. "I may be in very poor health, but I won't be the first to leave. Dead or alive. No, I'll bury you."

"Hush up, you old fool. I want to go back to my Agatha Christie."

"So you can learn new ways to try to murder me?"

"Once upon a time," Delphinia began to sing softly, "there was a little boy who had a little—"

"Shut your mouth, you dried up old rip."

"Yes, Henry, I may be dried up, but I dried up in my old age. Not when I was young, like you."

Henry leaned back and sighed. His thought process had become as ineffectual as his body. Meekly, he replied, "Delphinia, we can never undo the past. But I try each day of my life to put some of the horror out of my mind. Just one day, let the past stay where it belongs, away back there."

"Away back where, Henry? Your past is always in front of you. It always will be as long as there is the Wisteria. And your Bleeding Hearts and Lady's-slippers."

"Some day I'm gonna get rid of those vines. You'll see."

"You're redundant and boring, so just take a nap."

A pernicious silence descended upon the acrimonious siblings. Henry, fearful to close his eyes, looked toward the vines. A chill touched him. He hugged his shawl tighter around his shoulders.

Delphinia broke the silence. She spoke more to herself than to Henry.

"I remember when the houses were new around here. It was such a pretty street. A short block. The pavement was so nice and smooth. I used to love to go roller-skating on it. Our house and Dorothea's were the only single-family houses. I don't think you could call hers a house, though. It

20

was more like a shack left over from the farm that used to be here. It was an eyesore. Like those ugly old dump trucks that used to park across the street in the city garages. Do you ever think about them, Henry?"

Henry ignored her question.

"Henry, I'm asking you if you think about the garages?"

"Don't start up, Delphie. You know I've spent my whole life trying to forget. And so should you."

"It was a long time ago, but I still like to think about those days. I remember who used to live in every house. The Campbell's in the green and white one, with the Rizzo's on the second floor. The Ryan's and the Thurber's in the brown one. Henry, do you remember when the Ryan's got evicted? Their furniture was put on the street. Momma warned us to stay away from them because she was afraid we'd bring cockroaches home. Let's see now, the Paloma's and the De Rose's lived in the gray one. They're all gone now. Just us and the Neely sisters remain. I don't know any of the new people. All the old ones died or moved away. Then, of course, Dorothea and Dandy didn't last too long to begin with."

"You're determined to torture me to death, aren't you? Didn't I just ask you to let it rest?"

"You mean, let 'them' rest don't you?"

"Yes! Yes! Yes! Have it your way," Henry fumed.

"We used to call ourselves the Three D's," Delphinia persisted. "We had our own little secret club. Dorothea, Dandy and me, Delphinia. And of course, you had to tag along with me everywhere I went."

"I didn't tag along," Henry defended himself.

"You did too. You tagged along to the fields. You even used to follow us girls when we went over to Dandy's to go to the bathroom."

"I did not tag along. You used to take me to the bathroom with you girls. I remember things too. When I had to go, you and those girls would watch me. You'd point and snicker."

"I didn't take you anywhere. You were always there."

"Momma made me go. And you know it."

"But Momma didn't make you take your pants down."

"Dorothea did," Henry yelled. "I didn't know what that bastard had in mind. I was only six years old, you bitch." Henry struggled to his feet. Faltering, he walked to the porch rail, leaned forward and gripped the railing with both hands. His head rested against the sinewy, contorted Wisteria vines. Through an opening in the vines, Henry watched Doctor Boland park his car.

"The doctor's here. Don't go acting in front of him like the sweet thing you ain't and never will be. Just leave us alone."

"I'll think about it," Delphinia answered, then hurried to the steps at the end of the porch to meet the doctor.

Henry, frustrated by his sister's extreme behavior, tapped his head against the Wisteria vines, mumbling obscenities toward his sister.

"Yoo hoo, Doctor!" Delphinia called out as Doctor Boland made his way up the shrub-lined path. "Henry is here on the porch."

Doctor Boland, a robust man of fifty, waved and smiled. Streaks of silver singed his red hair. His bearing was pleasant and amiable. He greeted Delphinia with a squeeze of the hand.

"It was such a lovely day, I wheeled him out here. I thought he'd enjoy the fresh air."

Delphinia slipped her arm under the doctor's as they walked toward Henry.

"You are the best nurse I could prescribe for anybody, Miss Compton. I only wish there were ten more of you," he patronized the pretentious Miss Compton.

The ever-perceptive Delphinia smiled the smile of self-gratification when she observed the shocked expression that came across the doctor's face when he saw Henry standing with his head in the vines.

"Henry, what are you doing? You'll scratch your face against those rough vines. Besides you should be sitting in your chair, not up exerting yourself.

Henry turned and faced them. "I only took two steps. That's all it takes to get from there to here." Henry extended his arm and pointed to diagram his movement. "And that was just a second ago as you pulled up to the curb. How much can I just sit?"

"That's all well and good. But tell me, Henry, is there a reason for you tapping your head against the vines? Do you have a pain?"

The doctor applied his fingertips to Henry's temples, then ran them down the side of his face to his neck and throat.

"Does it somehow relieve pressure or make you feel better in some way?"

Delphinia walked around Henry's spilled lunch. "Doctor, I've told him over and over that he should be very careful. You can see he's had trouble just trying to hold his eating utensils." Just look at this mess. He's spilled his whole lunch all over the floor." Her arms dramatically opened wide to emphasize her point. I don't know how I'll get that soup stain out."

"Delphie, for God's sake, shut the hell up."

"When that happens, Doctor, he gets so upset, he raises his blood pressure. I had to leave the mess right where it is, because he argues with me every time I go to help him. It thwarts him so to be the way he is."

"You never quit, do you?"

"No, I don't. The doctor should know. Every time I turn my back, you're up and around, leaning against that vine and banging your head. Like now. I'm so afraid you'll get it caught in one of the openings and scratch your eyes out or something."

"Your sister's right, you know." Doctor Boland put his arm around Henry. "Miss Compton, will you help me get him back to his chair?"

"Delphinia, don't you touch me." Henry commanded.

24

"There's no reason to be so discourteous to your sister, Henry. After all she's done for you. I'm surprised at you."

"I don't want her to touch me, Doc."

"Well, I need her to get you back where you belong. Now, straighten up and cooperate."

"Oh, I'll cooperate, Doc. But I don't want any help from her. Just give me a hand and I'll be okay. I can make it back to the chair if you just let me lean on you."

"I apologize for my brother's behavior, Doctor. I hope you understand. He's been like this for the last few weeks."

"That ain't so, Delphinia. Why say such a thing? Don't listen to her, Doc. Even you'd go crazy if you had to put up with her twenty-four hours a day, every day of your life."

Doctor Boland winked at Delphinia and motioned her to back away and let him guide Henry to his wheelchair.

"Ain't you going to pick up this mess on the floor, Delphinia?"

Doctor Boland eased Henry down into his wheelchair. "Me and the Doc here could've fallen and broke our asses."

A chagrined Delphinia quickly knelt down and picked up the some of the debris. Doctor Boland, embarrassed for Delphinia, tried to ignore the bantering.

"Might as well get ready and roll up your sleeve, my friend."

"Right or left sleeve, Doc."

"Right will do." Doctor Boland handed his patient a thermometer. "Put this under your tongue." Doctor Boland adjusted his stethoscope while Henry slowly rolled up his sleeve.

"May I get you a cup of tea, Doctor?"

"Thank you, Delphinia. I'll have to take a rain check. I'm running behind schedule."

Henry removed the thermometer from his mouth and handed it to Doctor Boland.

"How is it? Normal?"

"A little elevated." The doctor wiped down the thermometer with cotton and alcohol and returned it to his bag.

"Delphinia, why are you standing there holding those dirty dishes? Take them the hell out of here. And don't come back. We can get along without you."

Delphinia glanced at Doctor Boland. She was confident that her brother's bizarre conduct had registered with the Doctor. She was counting on him to remember Henry's erratic behavior, if and when the time came. His was the professional testimony required to explain Henry's sudden death. Her eyes darted quickly to meet the stares of her brother. Delphinia maliciously sneered.

Henry fathomed the depth of loathing his sister held for him and realized immediately the game of words they had been playing all these years was no longer a game of sibling rivalry but a strategy. He knew Delphinia was maneuvering to kill him. But how? When? He was terrified.

As Doctor Boland wrapped the blood-pressure band about Henry's arm, Henry was conscious of his sister sinisterly encircling him as she made her way back into the house. How would she retaliate for being humiliated by his command to pick up his mess and leave the porch? His heart pounded so rapidly he quivered.

Doctor Boland squeezed the blood pressure pump.

Inside the house, Delphinia quietly set the tray on a small table near the entranceway. Determined not to miss a word between the two men, she leaned toward the screen door and cocked her head.

"What's the verdict, Doc?"

"Not so good, Henry. It's shot up. Way up."

"I feel okay though."

"This thing is a silent attacker."

"So you're saying I should be wary of a silent attacker, huh, Doc?"

"If you don't take precautions, they'll get you every time."

Henry folded his hands in his lap and put his head down. After a moment of silent contemplation, he raised his head and searched deep into Doctor Boland's eyes.

"I guess I'd better be on my guard, then."

Doctor Boland perceived a solemnity in Henry's composure that conveyed some kind of urgency.

"Don't worry, Henry, we'll keep it under control. It will be all right as long as we keep our eye on it." Doctor Boland tried to calm Henry's fear of dealing with another setback in his long, ongoing illness.

27

"Believe me, it's not the blood pressure I have to fear. But I do appreciate your making this house call just for me, Doc."

"Oh, it's no bother. I have two or three confined patients in this area. They aren't able to make it into the office. Getting out and doing house calls once in a while kind of keeps me in my place. Lets me remember that it's all part of the business of being what's called a General Practitioner. When Delphinia called earlier in the week, she sounded quite concerned. I can understand why, since I got a chance to see your behavior. Your depression is causing you to react toward her in a very rude and unpleasant manor."

"My sister called you? Now, why the hell did she do that? I never asked her to call you. She's got something up her sleeve. I'm really in danger. I better be careful."

"Is that a way to talk about someone who cares about you. That good woman worries about you, Henry. You know, you're very fortunate to have a sister like her looking after you."

"Believe me, Doc, you don't know the half of it. She's an asp. Sweetness disguises her venom. Doc, do you know what it says in the dictionary about my sister's lovely, flowery name, Delphinia? It says it's part of the buttercup family. You know, the kind that kid's stick under their chins to see if it casts a yellow shadow. Sounds nice, doesn't it? But as you read further on, it says that they're perennial and erect. Just like my sister. Always carrying herself straight. Ever notice when she walks, how she walks? She pulls her shoulders back. Then read

28

a little more and it says "they have showy spikes, and include several more that are poisonous." Just like my sister. A blooming bouquet that kills."

"Henry, I think you'd better find something better to do than reading the dictionary to find new words to insult your sister. It's unhealthy. You're sending you're pressure sky high. I'm going to have to give you a shot to calm you down."

"I don't want to go to sleep, Doc. Like you said, I got to watch for that silent attacker."

"It won't put you to sleep, only calm you down a little. Since you aggravated your old trouble—and you know your last heart attack landed you flat on your ass—with your history, it's going to take some time to get you on the road to recovery. I'm warning you, you have got to be extremely careful. You don't want to go through another stroke do you? If you keep going the way you are, you'll end up in the hospital again."

"If it'd get me a week's vacation away from her, I'll take it."

You should worship the ground she walks on, Henry. She's really a giving woman. Now, unbutton your shirt. I want to give a listen to your chest."

"Doc, I know my sister. I also know a few things about you just by looking at the 'Morse code' lines on your face."

"Now, quiet down and take a deep breath and cough."

Henry sat motionless and behaved like a chastised child as the doctor listened to his heart and lungs. He coughed right on cue.

"Button your shirt, Henry. I've finished. Where the hell did you get some of your down-country sayings?" The doctor folded up his stethoscope. "I'm gonna bite. What do you mean by 'Morse code' lines?"

"I mean that those lines on your face telegraph you're fast approaching late middle age. I suspect that, after college, all you doctors aspire to achieve that late-middle-aged look. Not old age, but that unique, distinguished look of middle age. Where the young cotton up to you and the old respect your advice because you're old enough to know everything and young enough to know the latest medical updates and techniques. That way, you got the market covered so both the young and the old can put all their trust and faith in you. Right, Doc?"

"No, you're not right." Doctor Boland shook his head and laughed. "You know, I got your number. You can't pull that 'old man in a wheelchair' act on me. You are a very opinionated, closed-minded son of a bitch, so stop emitting your homegrown horse shit on me. I think you just try to see how far you can go before you get my dander up. Well, it won't work."

"I like you, Doc. You don't pull any punches and you talk down to earth. Well anyway, even though I didn't call you, I guess I got to pay you. You're gonna have to send me the bill. I don't want to ask that old viper to get my wallet."

"Henry, you're paying for my advice, so listen and lighten up. Don't be such a hard-assed bastard. Show a little kindness to you sister."

Doctor Boland went through the ritual of swabbing Henry's arm, then reached into his bag for a syringe and a phial of serum. "She's a wonderful human being. You've got her all wrong."

Henry watched intently, as the doctor plunged the needle into the glass phial. He winced as he saw the orange-colored liquid fill the hypodermic vial. "You gonna give me all of that? I told you, I don't want to be put out."

"It's a very mild dose."

Henry closed his eyes tightly as the needlepoint pricked his arm. He didn't open them until Doctor Boland withdrew the needle and swabbed the punctured area again.

"It's good to talk to someone else besides the deadly Delphinia, so I guess your visit helped me, Doc."

Doctor Boland packed his bag and closed it. The snap of the doctor's bag brought Delphinia out from behind her hiding place.

"How's the patient's chart reading today, Doctor? Better, I hope." Delphinia was still playing the nurse's role.

"I have a new prescription for him. I'll phone it in and have it delivered. But with a nurse like you, we'll have the patient off our hands in no time at all."

"She may be off my hands first, Doc."

"Henry, your childish behavior has created one awkward situation here. Let me tell you that I resent being used by you just to vent your idiosyncrasy. Stop blaming your sister for a predicament you initially brought upon yourself."

Startled by Doctor Boland's stinging rebuke, Henry mumbled a half-hearted, "You got me wrong, Doc. 'Cause I say what I mean and I mean what I say, even if you take offense. You don't really understand what's going on here."

"There is nothing going on here. You're just enjoying your cantankerous old self, and you know it."

Delphinia was quite encouraged by the little melodrama she'd manipulated. She was extremely pleased that Doctor Boland was visibly struck by her brother's unusual behavior. The timing was perfect. The dialogue between the principals was memorable. She smiled modestly and took Doctor Boland's sleeve to accompany him toward the steps.

"Again, I must beg forgiveness for him, Doctor. Sometimes he gets so mean and depressed, his behavior becomes unpredictable. I don't know what he'll do next. It's gotten so I'm afraid he'll harm himself again in some gruesome way. Like he did before. I couldn't go through that again."

"Don't worry, Miss Compton. With the help of the medication I've prescribed and the injection, the old mule will soon be resting quietly. Just a few things before I leave. Give him an alcohol rub to lower his temperature. The needle will slow him down. And the prescription will make him sleep soundly tonight. Keeping us hopping is his vocation. He has nothing to occupy his time. Try to get him interested in a hobby. Or have some visitors drop by to keep him company. That'll get him out of these dark, depressing moods."

"Good-bye, Doctor. Thank you for being so understanding."

Henry was waiting for Delphinia's return "That was quite a display of sisterly affection you put on for the doctor's benefit, Miss Nursey."

"There was a little boy who had a little thing, and then one day he cut it off with just one swing," Delphinia sang out.

Henry's lips began to twitch. Fury blazed from his eyes. In his frenzy, he lifted himself up to lunge toward Delphinia. But he could only manage a stifled cry.

. "I'll choke your wrinkled neck."

Delphinia grabbed his shoulders and pushed him down in his chair. "Poor Henry. Getting up is so difficult for you."

"Bitch! Bitch! Bitch!" Henry spewed with loathing.

Delphinia sang louder. "You can never swing. You ain't got that thing." She waved her arms and danced around her brother.

"Stop your god damn crazy dancing."

She stopped in front of him and placed her hands on her hips. "What's the matter, little brother? Does seeing me dance and wave my arms make you wish you had something you could wave around and get up and dance about?"

"You are one goddamned crazy woman."

"Is 'god damn' the strongest word you can use? You can't even half swear like a man. Your words are as emasculated as you are."

"Your foul ways got us where we are today."

"Stop hiding behind your phony puritanical ways. You knew what was happening right up to the end."

"I didn't know anything about anything then. And you know it. You took my hand and lead me, step by step, into that empty garage. I remember how you and Dandy, the both of you, yanked on my belt buckle, trying to unloosen it. You and that bastard, Dorothea, planned it all. Dorothea said, 'Let's do what the big people do.' How in the hell did I know what big people do. I was only six years old. And when you made me lay on top of her, I didn't know what was happening to me. I was so scared. And you, my sister, just giggled." Henry's voice trailed off. He closed his eyes and turned his head away from Delphinia's indifferent stare. "I've gone over that scene in my mind's eye many times. The way I remember it, you helped them. I'll never understand why you betrayed me the way you did."

Delphinia folded her arms and raised her chin. "I'll always relish the memory of that scene too. I remember your snow-white ass wiggling on her belly. You crying and Dorothea bouncing up and down, trying to get you to use your little thing. You, with your wide-eyed innocence. Your first and last time."

"I was all innocence right up 'til you took me home to Momma. You couldn't wait to burst out and tell her what I had done." Henry tried to mimic the high, whiny tonal sound of the child, Delphinia. 'Momma, Brother put his thing between Dorothea's

34

legs.' Then you giggled. Why do you always giggle? Is it because you know how evil you are?"

"I giggle because you amuse me. You pretend to be so piously incorruptible."

Henry paused and looked at his sister with pity. He tilted his head slightly, then brought a fist up to his lips and closed his eyes. He held his breath in an effort to regain some composure before he went on. "I remember Momma was standing over by the sink, chopping onions for supper. When she turned to us, tears were already streaming down her face. I'll never forget her scream. It was then I realized I must have done something very, very bad. Sinful. That was the moment any innocence I may have had left me forever."

Delphinia shook her finger in Henry's face. "Momma shook that knife, like this, in your face." Henry winced and turned his cheek but Delphinia was enjoying herself too much to notice. "I can hear her yelling, even to this day, she continued. "'I'll chop it off, do you hear me? You dirty, dirty little boy. You know what's going to happen to you, you bad, bad boy. It's gonna get rotten and fall off. Do you know that?'"

"Yes, yes, yes, I know, I know, Momma." Henry's voice rose in pitch. He stood up unaided and called out, "Momma. Don't cry. I'm sorry. I'm really sorry, Momma. I'll never do it again. Please, I promise, Momma. Don't cry, Momma. I'm sorry."

"You were always sorry. Sorry for everything. You're one of those sorry people. Making up excuses why you're alive. Just once, I'd like to hear you say, 'I'm glad I did it. I had fun doing what I did,' instead of crying, 'Delphie made me do it.' You screamed then and you scream now. You're as prissy now as you were then."

With each venomous word brother and sister hurled at each other, brutal memories began to surface of an afternoon somewhere in their arcane past. And now the enigma of that arcanum afternoon leapt from its abyss to celebrate in its evil misdeed.

"Yeah, a lot of screaming went on in the Compton house that day. And a lot of blood spilled on the floor, blood that won't go away. Will it, Sister dear? No matter how much you scrub and scrub, it's always there. The sad part, Delphinia, is that when we were kids, I loved you."

Henry took a step toward the porch railing and fell. Doctor Boland's mild sedative was slowly beginning to restrain his muscles.

Delphinia walked over and pulled Henry's wheelchair away from him. She threw his shawl at him and sat in the wheelchair. She leaned back and got comfortable. Her hands cuddled the wheel's guide. She began to turn the wheels. Slowly at first. The chair rolled forward.

"This isn't so bad." She backed up and maneuvered her way around the body of her brother. Gaining some speed, she rolled herself to the other end of the porch and back again, coming to stop a few inches from Henry's prostrate body. "I got the feel of it, Henry. It's great fun."

Henry rolled over on his stomach and began to crawl toward the porch railing. Delphinia wheeled herself after her brother. She touched him

36

with the toe of her shoe. "Go ahead and crawl, Henry."

"I saw you crawl, Sister. All the lights were on. You didn't want to stand up. Remember? It was the night you killed all the love in our family."

"You and your Daddy. You two always stuck together. I never liked him to come near me. He always smelled of tobacco and sweat. Well, I'm glad he's dead." She looked over at the Wisteria vines. "The vines. That's what Daddy was doing that day. He was digging the trench to plant the vines. He was full of dirt and mud. When he came into the kitchen, he wanted to know what all the yelling and screaming was about. I couldn't help but laugh when Momma made you tell him what a terrible thing you had done."

"He knew it wasn't my fault. He knew you were to blame. He wanted you to tell him why you let them do those things to me. He knew you girls planned the whole thing. He knew you did it to me."

"You're whining again, Henry. I remember Momma's outraged expression when he told her that she was getting so excited about nothing."

"Delphie, stop it."

Delphinia paid no mind to his plea. She persisted in her recitation. "Can't you just hear him? His voice had a kind of nasal sound. 'You're making too much of an issue, Peg. Let it die down, Peg. Let it die down. It'll pass, Peggy. So he got his first piece at an early age. It only goes to prove he's all boy. Like father like son.' Those were his exact words. I can hear him so clearly. I can see him now, trying to comfort Momma. Those dirty, grimy arms trying to embrace her." Delphinia scowled and shrugged her shoulders in disgust.

Henry crawled to the railing and pulled himself up. He leaned his thin, exerted body against the railing's wooden slats. His legs were shaking uncontrollably. He held the rail with whatever meager strength he could muster. He took a couple of deep breaths before he spoke. "Delphinia, please! No more. I'm getting tired."

Delphinia was ecstatic. She saw him not as her brother, but as her prey, wrapped in silk threads she spun to encase him. She reveled in his helplessness.

"When Momma heard those words she forgot she was holding the knife. She lunged at your Daddy and put the blade right through his belly."

"Oh, Delphie. You brought the whole thing on." His words came haltingly and slurred. He gulped for air and slumped on the floor.

Delphinia lowered her voice and spoke in a raspy, excited tone, further antagonizing her victim. "All hell broke lose then. Daddy lay on the floor, his blood oozing out and mixing with the dirt he dragged in on his boots." Delphinia rose up out of the wheelchair and walked to the railing. She reached out and touched the vines.

Henry, listless and motionless, remained on the floor, resting against the railing. "Poor Momma. You drove us, Delphie. You drove us. You just never could let things be."

Delphinia spoke out to the Wisteria vines. "There are some brittle twigs protruding along the main vines. We have not been taking care of

38

Daddy's Wisteria lately. I'll have to do something about that very soon." She looked down at her brother "Of course I couldn't let things be. Somebody had to do something. Momma couldn't move. She was so petrified."

"Poor Momma," Henry sobbed. "We didn't know what to do. The poor woman was in a state of shock. Because of you, her whole life had been shattered. Because of you, she accidentally killed her husband. She kept repeating over and over, 'What? What, Delphinia? What are you saying?' She couldn't understand what you wanted us to do with Daddy's body. When she was crying for help, it was God she was crying to, not you. We never were sure that Daddy was really dead. That thought has haunted me all these years.

"Of course he was dead. If we'd called an ambulance, the police would have put Momma in jail. We'd be graduates of one foster home after another. We did the right thing."

"You were only a girl. You don't know if he was really dead. If only she didn't listen to you. But instead, she let you, a twelve year old, take command of the situation. You insisted on burying him."

Henry's words were spaced and coming more slowly. The effect of the drug was nearing its potential. "You took over and turned the whole thing into a game, like we were playacting at burying a canary or a dead cat. Funeral. We played funeral. And you presided over the whole horrible episode. You got stronger with the excitement, while we shook with fear. 'Pull down the shades,' you ordered, 'and lock all the doors.' I was so scared that God would see us and punish us. I ran around the house and did everything you told me to do. We sat there in that darkened kitchen for what seemed an endless nightmare. We were afraid someone would knock on the door or come in unexpectedly. Then you told us to wait until midnight so nobody would see us drag Daddy's body out of the house and into the front yard."

"Well, it was dangerous. Someone could have seen us."

"Momma. Pitiful Momma. That frenzied woman dragged Daddy out of the kitchen, through the hall and out onto this porch."

"Don't think I wasn't frightened too. I was afraid Momma would go completely crazy and stab me with that knife."

"I've spent a lifetime wishing she had stabbed you instead of Daddy."

"You make me out to be so hardhearted. I was worried about you too. She could have killed both of us."

"Maybe that would have been the best solution."

"Don't talk like an idiot. I was the only one who had any wits about them. I had to think fast to save Momma from herself. We also had to wait until we saw that all the lights in the houses across the street were out so we could sneak out to dig the ditch deeper in one spot to fit him in better. The hedges out by the sidewalk helped to hide us too. And then again, it was past midnight when we started and almost dawn when I finished the job. You weren't much help at all."

"I tried to calm Momma the whole time you were out there. She kept asking me where you were and what you were doing. How was I to tell her you digging Daddy's grave deeper? Then she'd beg me to tell her that she was dreaming. It was horrible to see my mother like that."

"It wasn't easy, dragging him out of the house. Momma and I struggled to get him from the kitchen to the porch and down the steps to where he dug the trench for the vines. When you came out to help, you just knelt and watched as Momma and I pushed him into the hole. So you can say Daddy dug his own grave. He was dead, all right. Dead weight. And I, not you, covered him over. Like always, you were too sissy. But I made you plant those Bleeding Hearts and Lady's-slippers to build it up and make it look fuller."

Henry turned slowly and raised his eyes to meet Delphinia's. "I look at you and you seem to have a glow about you. Tell me, does talking about it give you a little thrill?"

Delphinia shrugged her shoulders and tilted her head, then let her shoulders drop. The smirk on her lips broadened into a smile.

"My God, Delphinia, you get a thrill talking about it."

Delphinia giggled. "To this day I'll never understand how the neighbors, and even Daddy's boss, believed that story I made up for Momma to tell about how Daddy deserted us."

"If there is a God, I thank him for taking Momma soon after that. Everyone said she died of a broken heart because Daddy left her." Henry stopped to take a deep breath. "She died of a broken heart all right." He stared his sister down. "A heart you pierced."

"Oh, aren't you the high and pious one. Have you forgotten your devilish deeds? Momma didn't die that soon after Daddy. What killed her was when Dorothea and Dandy were found with their heads bashed in and the police blamed it on a maniac. Momma knew you did it. That's what killed her. I may have pierced her heart. But you made it bleed." Delphinia threw her head back and giggled.

"You made me do it. You made me do everything. You planned everything. All I did was what you told me to do."

"You made me do it, you made me do it." Again, Delphinia mimicked Henry in her singsong manner. "It's so easy to blame someone else."

"I was only a little boy."

"You've been fooling yourself with that excuse for all these years. Own up to the fact that you were willing, able and went along with everything. You never really stood up and resisted. Look at you today. You're just cowardly."

"I wasn't willing. I did it only because you said we had to do it. Those girls, they knew what I did in the garage. You said they might tell on me. Their mothers would come here and upset Momma all over again."

"Yes. We had to kill them. Sooner or later, one of them would have squealed."

"You say it so cold-blooded. Did you ever feel any remorse?"

Delphinia ignored Henry's question as she continued. "I had one hell of a time getting Dandy to return to the vacant garage. She didn't want to come. She was quite apprehensive. And rightly so. But Dorothea was something else. She couldn't wait. She was ready for you to do it again. Well, you gave her something she never bargained for."

"I'm haunted by her dead eyes, staring up at me. I should've bashed your head in too that day. It would have saved me having to put up with you my whole life."

"Ah! You're not so innocent after all."

"Serves her right, though, for starting the whole thing. When Momma heard they were found dead, she started all over again with me. Saying it was dirty. Dirty. A dirty thing that I had down there. That it would cause me to do bad things all my life. I would die and suffer in hell because I had it."

Renewed by a sudden burst of energy, Henry bolted upright from the floor. He began to pound the air around him. That's when I decided to cut it off. Cut everything off." He screamed and collapsed at Delphinia's feet.

Delphinia rose and stood over her brother and in a flat, monotonous tone, spoke to him. "Henry, dear. I'm getting tired of playing our charade. It's wearing thin. After today, I'll be all alone in this house. I'm going to miss puttering around for you. But it's time, I think, for you to die."

Delphinia reached over the rail into the Wisteria vines. She felt for the sharp spur she had shown earlier to Doctor Boland. "Ah! There's the beauty." She snapped off the blooms of the obstinate shoot. "Nice," she murmured to the twisting vines. "Sharp. Strong enough to penetrate." She pushed and stretched an opening in the vines, fashioning them into a vise.

Delphinia knelt beside her brother. She put her arms under his shoulders. His puny form was heavier than she realized. She had to straddle him to get a firmer grip. Her skin prickled with adrenaline as she lay atop her brother. A tinge of electricity shot throughout her body. She lingered on him to enjoy the rapture a little longer.

As it waned, she wrestled to stand him over the railing, facing the Wisteria vines. She grabbed a fist full of his hair and turned him halfway around. Holding onto his hair, she pulled his head back and kissed him on his mouth. Henry flailed his arms in a defensive gesture. After she kissed him, she struggled to jam his head into the wide gap she had created in the vines. With her free hand, she reached into the vines and felt for the spur. Her fingers poked Henry's neck to locate his pulse. The throbbing of his pulse assured her of her mark. She placed the prickly spur on the palpitating target of her brother's throat. Then she carefully pressed his head with just enough pressure to allow the thorny spur to puncture his skin. She released her grip on Henry's hair and let his head limply fall. His fluid heritage spurted onto the entwined branches of the Wisteria. Delphinia softly giggled.

Henry opened his eyes and realized that his head was trapped in the Wisteria vine. He panicked and tried to pull free. The more he struggled, the deeper the briar penetrated. Henry had impaled himself.

As Henry twitched and jerked, Delphinia embraced her brother from behind, tightly clinging to him. Her body joined his in a convulsive rhythmic union, sharing in his final, supreme sensation. When the twitching and lurching ended, Delphinia laid her head upon her brother's back and listened for the silence of his exhausted heart.

"I told you that you would be the first to die and that I would bury you. I always keep my word." She whispered, softly, as she watched the red liquid run down along the Wisteria vine and drip onto the blossoms of the Bleeding Hearts and Lady's-slippers.

"Now your blood will mingle in the dirt with your precious daddy's."

Delphinia giggled.

***

MEMOIRS OF A CLEAVAGE STUFFER

During the early days of television when everything was done live, a special job was created for the medium that has now gone out of existence. For want of a better name, it was called the Cleavage Stuffer. I was the original cleavage stuffer on NBC's Jerry Lester's BROADWAY OPEN HOUSE, the first of the Late Night Shows. Today I cannot find a job in television because there is no demand for my expertise in that area of the business: a kind of peripheral backstage handyman. Not quite a prop man, but on the periphery.

As a cleavage stuffer, I would position myself in the wings or behind some scenery with my tools of the trade, a box of tissues, and inspect the cleavage of every woman that was about to appear on camera. After make-up powdered their faces and touched up their hair, the girls in the dancing line, as well as any noted woman guest star, would stand before me for cleavage inspection.

I applied my trade on some of the most beautiful and glamorous women in the world. The gowns and dresses they wore were designed by famous designers and were probably priced in the four- and five-figure dollar amounts. But as the cleavage stuffer, I had final absolute say as to whether the American public would be allowed to see them from neckline to hemline.

I especially enjoyed working with the girls in the chorus line. They would linger and joke around until the last minute, pulling and stretching their necklines, daring me to stuff the tissue. The band would start and I would be frantically stuffing tissues as each girl passed before me, dancing her way into living rooms and bedrooms all over North America.

I always respected and complied with the wishes of anyone who did not want my assistance in covering their cleavage. I would willingly dispense a tissue to her, letting her decide how she wished to stuff it. Only one lady refused the motif of a cleavage tissue, and needless to say, she appeared on camera in either a facial close up or one that did not display her from the neck down. I don't hold a grudge against her. She was within her rights. So many things have changed over the years, except the unnamed lady has never lost that Hungarian accent.

For a young man attending college in the day and working in experimental television at night, I was given tremendous power. By today's standards, I was sanctioned to break all kinds of constitutional laws. But in those hurly-burly days of live vaudeville-style song-and-dance shows, it was an accepted unwritten rule of propriety. Hollywood had its Hayes Office, and network television, its Cleavage Stuffer.

Dagmar, blonde, buxom, statuesque and endowed with a guileless charm was the main attraction on BROADWAY OPEN HOUSE. She was the Dolly Parton of early TV. She would do a stand-up comic routine of reading poetry while the top banana Jerry Lester and his beanbag style of comedy used her as his foil. It was her wit and sense of humor that teased America into staying up late to watch TV.

Famous designers, well known New York department stores and lesser known coutures, all vied for the opportunity to gown and clothe Dagmar for her on-camera appearances. They did this gratis just to hear Dagmar say, "Do you like my dress?" as the opening lines to her routine. After the audience roared its approval she would mention the designer's name.

One night, a beautiful black-sequined, strapless gown was delivered. I accepted the dress and hung it in Dagmar's dressing room, then went about my business of cleavage stuffing. Dagmar arrived later than usual and had not tried the dress on before the show. The show was minutes away from airtime when suddenly Dagmar let out a yell for me to come to her dressing room fast. An emergency had arisen: the dress did not fit. It was not only too tight to fit into without bursting the seams, but the bra size was several cups sizes too small, and to add insult to injury, the bra was padded. If there was anything that Dagmar did not need it was padding in her bra.

She had the dress half on and half off when I got there. She had pulled the dress up over her waist but could not move it up any higher. She needed someone strong to stand behind her to pull the dress up and to zip the zipper as we moved the fabric inch by inch up and over until it was high enough to cover her cleavage. I pulled and zipped as she tore and ripped out lining, sequins and bra padding while squeezing and stuffing herself into a gown sewn together for a kewpie doll.

Meanwhile, the audience was filing into the studio and the band was tuning up while we were redesigning Dagmar's gown. The clock was running and show time was getting closer and closer and Jerry Lester was pounding on the dressing room door, demanding to know if Dagmar was alone or if she had a man in there with her. He was livid that Dagmar had locked her dressing room door and denied him access. He insisted that he be let in immediately.

Dagmar and I paid him no mind but kept working feverishly. It was no easy job we set out to accomplish. It took its toll in sweat and tears. I was sweating and panting; she was sobbing and exhausted. We completed our mission with dignity and, as they say in the trade, good taste. There was never a moment of indiscretion or embarrassment. Dagmar thanked me and unlocked the door to let me out. I left her to face the wrath of Jerry Lester.

When Jerry Lester saw me leaving Dagmar's dressing room, he was furious. Why, I don't know. I can only guess that it was professional one-up-man-ship: here was the most famous woman in television locked in her dressing room with the lowliest of employees, while he, the chagrined star, was left on the outside begging to be let in.

On the next payday, NBC cleavaged me from its list of employees by stuffing a pink slip into my envelope, thereby sending my particular job the way of the Bean Bag. But do I care? Not when I

have that shinning moment of being alone with
Dagmar and being who we were and doing what we
did and doing it together in that era that was alive
with live television.

***

MERRY CHRISTMAS, SANTA CLAUS

On Cold days, I like to take my 'daily constitution,' as Harry Truman used to call it, in a climate-controlled shopping mall. To me, the next best thing to walking in the woods and breathing in the fresh air is walking through the mall. I love the smell of coffee brewing and pastry baking, mixed with the odors from the perfume counters. For me, the first sign of Christmas is not a snowflake drifting down from its secret hiding place in the sky or receiving the season's first greeting card. It's watching the window dressers change the world from Thanksgiving's orange and rust to the red and green of Christmas dreams. I especially enjoy the wonderful wide-eyed awe that comes over the faces of children as they stand in line waiting to meet and talk to Santa Claus.

Last Christmas I was just settling myself down on my favorite bench in the town mall not too near and not too far from Santa's throne when I received a sharp jab to my right arm. I ignored the obtrusive gesture. After a moment or two, I felt another jab and heard, "Hey, mister, what's your name?"

I was annoyed. I didn't turn my head. I just kept staring straight ahead at the children in line. Then in a brusque unpleasant tone still staring straight ahead, I answered the question with a question. "What's your name?"

"John," the voice replied.

"Same as mine." I turned to tell the annoying John politely but firmly to stop poking and asking questions. But the words died before they reached my lips. Sitting beside me was a smiling young man whose beard was just beginning to shadow his complexion. He wore the same familiar expression of awe as those children waiting to tell Santa their Christmas wishes.

John was an adolescent destined to reach manhood and yet always have the trust and innocence of a very young child. I didn't know what to do next. The boy's charm and straight forwardness had thrown me for a loss. So I smiled and winked the way old men do when they don't know what to say to a youngster.

John returned the smile and tried to wink but only succeeded in closing both his eyes. He reached over and gently stroked my beard. I was uncomfortable and pulled away.

"You have a white mustache and white beard just like Santa Claus."

"I know. Sometimes people call me Santa Claus."

John's eyes widened. "You really are Santa Claus! I can tell. When do you put on your Santa clothes?"

"On Christmas Eve. I dress up for my grand...." Again, I stopped mid-voice. I had to collect my thoughts and regain my composure. It was obvious from John's expression that he truly believed I was Santa Claus.

"John, let me explain. I'm not who you think I am. Santa Claus is up there." I pointed to the jovial man with the fake beard.

"No. That's one of his helpers. My Mom told me."

I was caught between two worlds, John's and mine. Christmas for John and other young children is the age-old myth of the midnight ride and eight tiny reindeer. This was one time that a smart-aleck old man's smart-aleck remark had outsmarted him.

"I wrote you what I want for Christmas." John was emphatic. "It has a red button and you push it, then it answers you back. Are you going to bring it to me, Santa?"

I was not about to upset this young man's world and tell him an old man's world was playing a game with him. He would never understand such cruel deception. I had to find a way to end this conversation. It had to be abrupt yet gentle. I didn't want to, but I had to patronize the boy.

"If your mom and dad said you could have it, I'm sure you will find it under your Christmas tree on Christmas morning."

"Here comes my mom now."

A smartly dressed woman laden with Christmas wrapped boxes and shopping bags came towards us. My pulse began to pound against my temples. If only the blaring sound system could've enveloped me and transported me somewhere far, far away.

I took a deep breath and closed my eyes. The mall with all its hustle-bustle suddenly evaporated. I saw myself as a hunched-over old codger sitting on a bench surrounded by over-decorated Christmas trees.

John's mother held out the shopping bags for her son to take.

"Mom, this is my friend."

I heard love in a boy's voice. Though it was meant for Santa Claus, I was jealous. I wanted it to be for me.

In his fervor John, reached over to stroke my beard again. His mother guided John's arm away from me, advising him not to touch people. She started to apologize when John excitedly interrupted her. "But Mom, it's okay. He's Santa Claus!"

From my sitting position I sheepishly looked up at John's mother.

"I'm sorry, Missus. I can't explain how it happened, but I think I've led him to believe I'm Santa Claus."

My voice never rose above a whisper. I was certain she knew she was in the presence of a fool.

"Momma, I told him I wanted the thing with the red button. You know, the one that answers you back when you push it."

I looked at John and then at John's mother and managed a feeble response. "I told him that if his mom and dad said it was all right, then he would find his present under his Christmas tree on Christmas morning."

After a moment of silent contemplation, the gracious lady replied, "If John asked for the thing with the red button, then I'd like you to deliver it to him, Santa." She smiled in my direction then

54

motioned for John to rise and get ready to leave. He stood up and took some packages from his mother. I was surprised he was quite tall. When he extended his hand, I reached out and clasped it tenderly and touched it to my beard.

That young man embraced this old man and said, "I love you, Santa."

With those words, there was no more jealousy. A friend cannot feel jealousy toward a friend. I wanted John to know I truly am his friend.

"I love you too, John."

Just before they disappeared into the holiday throng, John turned and waved. His voice rose above the din. "Merry Christmas, Santa Claus."

"Merry Christmas, John." I waved and let John go out of my sight and into my life."

*

Epilogue: The words "Humility, I feel thy sting" kept running through my mind as I watched John and his mother mingle with the other shoppers. I was so absorbed in my daily walk, my Christmas, my world, that I didn't have the courtesy to look at this boy when he first spoke to me. Being in John's presence made me question whether I'm a caring person with Christmas in my heart or just an observer of the Christmas pageantry. Does my Christmas spirit come from pretty ribbons and bows and all the pagan trimmings? Do I hear only the melody of the Christmas Carol and not the message. The elusive Christmas spirit is me and how I represent myself to John and everyone else. Once I begin to truly live what I profess to believe, the

Christmas spirit will always be with me. Although they were out of sight I gave one last wave.

"I love you, John. I will forever."

***

CIRCUS HOUSE

An icy zephyr swept past my face on that hot summer day and a chill touched my shoulders as I stood before the house we were moving into. It wasn't like any other house I'd ever seen. It was built behind a three-storied, nine-family tenement row house and painted a humiliating gray. It exuded no warmth or cheeriness. Our new house was a house without pride or dignity. It seemed to whisper shame and sadness. We were to live on the first floor of the two-story building. Louisa and Jocoab, old family friends and owners of the house, occupied the flat upstairs. The previous tenants had moved out quite unexpectedly.

My sister, Helen, entered the house first. She looked under the sink and poked into the dish closet. "Momma, I'm looking for cockroaches."

"That's a big help, Helen. Be careful you don't stick your hand in any mousetraps. See your brother Chase doesn't get into any mischief."

I'm the eldest. I'm called Cyrus after my father's father.

When Momma entered the kitchen, she was surprised to find a round kitchen table and four chairs "My goodness! I never expected anything as lovely as this. Look, Cyrus, it's solid oak."

Louisa came down with a cold pitcher of iced tea. "Are you doing all right? It's such a hot day for moving. Here's something cool for you."

"Thank you, Louisa, and thank you so much for the lovely kitchen table and chairs. Cyrus and I won't have to tote that old kitchen set of mine. This is so much nicer."

"Oh, don't thank me. Thank the family who lived here before. They moved out so fast. They said there was no room on the wagon. They must have money to waste."

"It's almost like new. I guess that's my good fortune.

"I'm sure things will work out well for you from now on."

"I'm looking forward to starting over in a new place. I really don't know what I would have done if I hadn't my Cyrus to lean on. He's been my strength."

"Yes, he's so level-headed for a young boy. He'll be a good man some day." Louisa smiled at me.

"I know he will." Momma put her arm around me and brushed the hair from in front of my eyes. "My Cyrus has had to grow up so fast. He's become the man of our family at fifteen."

I wanted to hug her and tell her how much I loved her. But grown up sons don't do things like that, especially when other people are around.

Without Jocoab and his horse and wagon, the move would not have been possible. For an extremely tall and skinny man, Jocoab was very strong. We were all moved before darkness.

Sometime during the night I awoke to flashing lights and rumbling sounds reverberating throughout the house. The shattering noise was unbearably loud. I thought it was thunder and lightning. I got up to look out the window to see if it was raining. But the sky was cloudless and the stars were bright. My brother who shared the bed with me was sound asleep. I saw nothing unusual, so I climbed back in bed. When the noise finally faded away, I closed my eyes and drifted back to sleep. I awoke again at dawn to the sounds of more rolling and rumbling. This time it was coming from the kitchen. I jumped out of bed, pulled on my pants and ran down the hall to find Momma struggling to push the kitchen table toward the middle of the room.

"Why did you push this table up against the wall, Cyrus? You know a round table doesn't look right shoved to one side of a room."

"I didn't push that table over there, Momma."

"You mean it wasn't you last night flashing the lights on and off? And the rumbling noise! It was atrocious. I was sure you were up and about rearranging some things. That's why I didn't get out of bed. Then this morning to find this."

"Momma, I didn't do it. I heard the noise last night too. I thought it was a storm. I even got up to see if it was raining. All I saw was moon and stars."

"Even though the middle leg has rollers, it took all my strength to shove it back to the middle of the room. How in the world did this happen? Somebody had to move it. It didn't get there by itself. Who could it have been if it wasn't you?

"Maybe somebody came in during the night to play a joke."

"Cyrus, don't say that. I'm afraid to even think about what's going on."

"Maybe there was some kind of earthquake."

"I never heard of an earthquake in this part of the country."

I got down on my hands and knees to survey the floor. "The floor isn't slanted, Ma, so it didn't roll over there by itself."

"I've got to hurry and fix breakfast. You can't be late for work either."

I work at Schlank's Grocery store full time in the summer and after school the rest of the year. Momma works as a maid.

"We'll worry about the table tonight. It's Saturday. Mrs. Mortonson asked me to stay late tonight. I don't know what time I'll be home. Here's a dime. Get ten cents' bologna for lunch. I hope we'll be all right in this house, Cyrus," she whispered as she handed me the coins.

"Cyrus," Chase greeted me when I returned home that evening, "there's a real old lady on the porch of the big building. She's smoking a glass jar filled with water. Look out the door. You can see her. See the hoses?"

The old woman sat cross-legged on the floor, holding a hose and blowing smoke in our direction. She saw us and motioned for us to join her.

"I'm not going." Chase moved behind me. "I'm too scared. Don't go, Cyrus."

I was scarred too, but curiosity made me cross the yard, climb the flights of stairs and join the old lady.

"Allo, boy. You name Cyrus. I Madame Verolga."

She had a kind of funny cracking voice. I never heard an accent like hers before. It didn't sound German or Italian. She wore a ring on every finger. Even her thumbs. And lots of beads around her neck. There was a diamond stuck on one side of her nose. I never saw anyone dressed like that ever. A blue silk shawl covered her head and her green dress covered her whole body down to her bare feet. I didn't know what to say, so I just stood there.

"You want try smoke tobacco?" She offered me a hose.

Fascinated, I gazed at the many colored petals drifting and dancing through the water bubbles. Maybe I was hypnotized by the curling and climbing of the petals, because I never hesitated; usually I have to be coaxed into doing anything so forbidden. Before I realized what I was doing, I took the hose and put it to my lips. I had never even tried to smoke a cigarette in my life. I think the old lady was wise to my trying to imitate what she was doing. However, she remained silent and went on smoking. I gulped the smoke too fast and deep so that I choked. Embarrassed, I tried again and slowly sipped the smoke. The old lady smiled at me with her eyes. Chase peeked from behind a tree, trying to see what the old lady and I were doing.

"How did you know my name?"

"I know lot things. I know why you move Circus House. You circus people."

What a strange thing to say. I thought she was crazy. "I don't understand what you mean by 'circus people.'"

"That house Circus House. Circus people make it. I circus lady. All people in house circus people."

"Louisa and Jocoab aren't circus people. They're my mother's friends."

"They circus. Louisa Papa, he boss. Own circus. Louisa and Jocoab work circus long years past."

A man came out of the house and sat beside the old woman and picked up a hose and started to smoke. "Hey, boy. You know what this call?" He pointed to the bowl.

I shook my head. "No."

"It's call Hookah. You know what name that is?" He pointed to the hose I held.

"No," I said. "It's pretty fancy with all the designs drawn on it."

"It's name Narbeesh. You should know what you hold in hand and put on lip. In my country, we sit 'round and smoke. Make new friends this way. My name Chakka."

"What country do you come from?"

"We circus people from Syria."

"Everybody in the whole building?"

"No. Come from Romania, Turkey, Syria, Russia, Italia, Ethiop'a, Espana. Whole world. Circus people."

"I don't know of any circuses around here. Is one coming to town?"

"No circus yet. Louisa and Jocoab let circus people stay here when they no work or circus run out money. Come here. Resting 'while."

He said he was a gypsy violinist for Demalda, the Belly Dancer. The old lady was his mother who read palms and tarot cards. She also had a crystal ball.

"You know people who live in Circus House before you and you Mama move in?"

"No. I didn't know them. Louisa said they only lasted six months."

Madame Verolga interrupted. "They no stay because they no circus people, but Louisa tell lie. They stay three day. Then swoosh, they go. Circus people understand. Circus people stay."

"Louisa wouldn't lie. We're not circus people either."

Chase had made his way up the stairs and stood beside me. He pulled at my sleeve and whispered in my ear. "Momma's home and she asked where you were. I didn't tell her. Let's go home now. I'm scared of that old lady.

I put the Narbeesh back on the Hookah base and stood up. "I've gotta go. My mother wants me."

"Come back, boy. We smoke tomorrow," the old lady said.

When we got home, Chase slammed the door and locked it. He never mentioned my smoking or talking with Chakka and the old lady.

I heard rumblings and scraping again that night as I lay in bed, somewhere off in a distant dream world. I was too exhausted from moving the day before and working all day to get up and investigate. When morning came, I expected to find Momma making Sunday breakfast. Instead, I found a note on the icebox, instructing me to fix some tea and hard bread with jam for Helen and Chase. Sunday or not, Momma had to work. I looked around the room to see if everything was just as we left it the night before. It seemed to be, except the table was not exactly in the middle of the room. It was off center. But Momma's note didn't mention anything about strange goings on with the table.

Chase and Helen and I were sitting around the table, wondering if there were any kids our age in the neighbor hood. We were startled to hear a faint tapping at the door. Chase glanced anxiously toward me.

"Suppose it's that old lady with the smoking bottle? Don't let her in, Cyrus. Momma's not here."

Helen laughed. "A smoking bottle? It's probably Louisa. I'll answer it."

"No. You sit with Chase. I'll get it."

"Why? What's wrong? Why are you boys so scared to open the door?"

"I'll tell you later. But right now, both of you stay where you are."

"I'm Nardelia." She held out a covered basket. "Take. These from Verolga. She say enjoy." Her voice was soft and pleasant but I couldn't look at her. I looked over her and to the side of her. I grabbed the basked out of her hands and rudely shut the door on her.

"I saw her face," Helen screamed.

"I did too." Chase, filled with fear, jumped from his chair. "I closed my eyes real quick. She scared me. I wish Momma was home. I hate this house. I want to go home to our real house. Why did Poppa have to die and leave us?" Chase began to cry.

Helen put her arms around him and held him until his sobbing stopped. I couldn't show them how scared I was.

"Don't even lift the napkin on that basket, Cyrus," my sister commanded.

"All right," I shouted, more angry with myself then with Helen and Chase. We got some waste paper from the moving boxes that were still lying about and turned the basket upside down to let its contents drop out.

"Don't touch it," warned Chase. "I won't eat that, even if I'm starving to death."

"It's some nice fresh fruit. Momma would be upset if she knew we threw out good food."

"Momma don't have to know," Helen replied. "If she finds out, we'll just say we ate it."

"You mean you'd lie?"

"I'd rather lie and ask God to forgive me than to eat that stuff and die of poison." My sister was getting distressed over the basket of fruit.

"Calm down, Helen. I'll return the basket later today. Okay? Now we'll wrap it real good in the paper then tie it up and put it in the trash."

Returning the basket gave me an excuse to visit the old lady. I wanted to hear the rest of what she had to say. Chakka met me on the stairs.

"You see Nardelia?"

I swallowed hard and nodded.

"Mama send her over. She frighten you?"

I nodded again.

"Never be 'fraid Nardelia. She polite, gentle-type girl. Her Mama was elephant rider. Very beautiful. She leave Nardelia when Nardelia baby. We keep her. When we go to circus again, Nardelia be big star all over world."

"How'd she get that way?"

"Come on porch. Mama make Hookah for us. You want?"

"Okay."

"Sit here." He placed a rug on the floor for me. "I get Mama and Hookah."

Chakka returned with the Hookah and Verolga. We sat around the Hookah as Chakka began the story about Nardelia.

"You ask 'bout Nardelia. You know, circus people very, how you say, superstish. We believe sign and omens. Nardelia, she like she is because of her Mama. Even if you not superstish, you must believe when I tell you true story. It happen just like I say. My Mama and Nardelia Mama, Tovara, work circus. Love same man, my father, Steffan. Steffan, he love Verolga. He love also Tovara at same time. He love so great, he must have both womans. My Mama, she know 'bout Steffan and Tovara. She no care. She love my father anyhow. But Tovara jealous woman. Had hatred for my Mama. When she see my Mama with child, she curse me, unborn child in my Mama. You too young understand all I say."

"No, no. I understand. I work in grocery store. I know what everything is about." I wanted him to know that I was a working man and old enough to understand what he was telling me. I also found myself unconsciously copying his manner of speaking.

"She put curse my Mama, that when she have baby," Chakka pointed his finger at his chest, "it come out look just like monkey from jungle. When gypsy woman say curse, that very, very bad. My Mama very, very sad long, long time. 'Til I born."

"What did Steffan do in the circus besides making babies?"

"My father was gypsy too. He musician, like me. But he leave trouble of womans to womans. Soon Tovara's belly began grow with child. She come to Verolga and ask forgive because she 'fraid curse will visit her. I come first. Healthy boy. My father happy to see boy. Then Tovara turn. She suffer very bad to let Nardelia out. Nardelia come two month two day after me. Tovara scream when she see baby. She push 'way. No want poor Nardelia. Nardelia look like fuzzy coconut with hair all over head, face, body." Chakka waved his hands in front of his face, then he touched his nose. "Nose small, like monkey." He drew his finger across his teeth. "When teeth grow, they grow one back of other like two row. She got five finger and thumb on both hands." He held out his hands and stretched his fingers wide. "Six toes too. He dropped his hands and pointed to his mother's uncovered toes.

My father, he cry. But he circus man. He know curse come true. Not for my Mama, for Tovara. So Nardelia, she go in circus show since little baby."

Chakka stopped to puff on the Hookah, and I did the same. The old lady continued the story of Nardelia.

"After Nardelia born, Tovara no want her. She leave us and go 'way. I tell Steffan I take Nardelia."

"What happened to Steffan?"

"My father, he die." Chakka bowed his head.

Nardelia came out and joined us. She sat quietly.

Chakka put his arm across her shoulders. "I love Nardelia, my sister."

When I went home, I took the fruit out of the trash box, unwrapped it and ate an apple. Momma came home around nine. I asked her how she found the table that morning. She was just about to answer me when we heard Louisa scream out my mother's name. Momma and I, followed by Helen and Chase, ran up the stairs to Louisa. The high-pitched shrieking came from the bathroom. Momma and I rushed into the small quarters to see Louisa sitting in a tub of sudsy water, shaking with laughter.

"Lydia, I can't get out of the tub and Jocoab is nowhere to be found." Her thickset shoulders bounced up and down, like waves on the ocean. She playfully slapped the sudsy water and splashed us.

Helen and Chase burst into laughter and tried to blow the suds back at her. I joined in the fun too. Momma was mortified. She turned and pushed us out of the room. But we didn't move fast enough because we were laughing so hard. So poor, thin Momma stood in front of the mountainous Louisa, waving her hands and shoeing us out of the room.

"Cyrus," Momma shrieked, "you take the children out of this room immediately."

"No, no, Lydia. We're going to need Cyrus' help. He's a strong, muscular young man. You can't lift me out of this damn tub all by yourself, especially if I can't give much help. I'm going to need the both of you to pull me out. I can't stop laughing. It's so funny."

I wanted to laugh too, but I saw the look on Momma's face. That look meant 'beware.'

"Don't be ashamed that the boy sees me with no clothes on. He's old enough to know that old ladies are different than young boys. It's not going to affect his manhood one way or the other." She kept laughing and talking as she winked at me. "Just think of it as saving an old lady's life, Cyrus. If it makes your Momma feel better, close your eyes, so you don't see what you're looking at." Louisa's flesh rippled and bounced with each explosion of laughter. "I hope your seeing me doesn't upset you, boy. I know you'd be enjoying yourself if I was a pretty young girl." Louisa threw her head back and let a convulsion of laughter escape her bulky flesh.

"Louisa! I'm shocked at your behavior," Momma chastised her friend.

Careful not to get soapsuds in her eyes, Louisa touched away her tears with the backs of her wrists. "You may call him a boy, Lydia, but he's well on his way to becoming a man. You know as well as I do that all men are boys for as long as they live. Anyway, I say let him stay. I need him now."

To my surprise, Momma relented, and together we worked very hard, pulling and tugging the giggling Louisa. We tugged with little success; Louisa's enormous body overflowed the tub. There were puddles of water all over the floor. Very little remained in the tub.

"Momma, why don't you rub her sides with a bar of soap? Maybe that will make her slide up when we pull on her arms."

"Lydia, this boy of yours has the right idea. Give me another bar of soap from the sink there. I think I'm sitting on the one I was using. I'll soap my whole body like a greased pig if I have to."

It took a lot of pulling and tugging but we finally got Louisa out of the tub. Louisa winked at me again and sniggered. She stood, dripping pools of water. I think I even winked back. Momma worked quickly to enfold her massive body in towels. Not so much to dry her but more for my being present.

"Louisa, if I live to be a hundred, I'll never forget this moment. I think it's the funniest thing I have ever seen in my whole life." Momma held her sides as she sat down in the window seat.

I just smiled. I still didn't dare move a muscle on my face. Louisa's getting stuck in her bath kind of brought Momma out of her depression.

70

I saw Momma laugh again, and for the first time in a long time, Momma and I shared a happy moment. I thought it best that I silently slip away.

I've known Louisa since I was a small boy. I guess, by knowing someone through a child's eyes, you see them for who they are and how warmly you feel toward them. I saw that Louisa was heavy, but I never really saw her as obese. Jocoab too. He's the skinniest man I've ever seen. I remembered what Madame Verolga had said. Like a bolt, it hit me. Louisa and Jocoab really are circus people! Louisa and Jocoab are the fattest lady and the skinniest man in the world.

Sitting alone with Momma in our kitchen later, I asked her about the table. She told me that she had heard the rolling and rumbling sounds the night before and found the table pushed over against the wall again this morning.

"Son, this thing baffles me. I don't know what to do about it."

"Maybe if we put the kitchen chairs around it, it will stay in place because the chairs might hold it there," I suggested.

Momma thought about that for a few seconds. "No. I think we should leave the chairs where we have them now, away from the table in their own places against the walls. If we circled the chairs around the table and it keeps moving, it might just take the chairs and scatter them as it moves about the room."

I agreed to leave it the way Momma wanted it and went to bed. I tossed and turned, unable to fall asleep. The mystery of the moving table and the novelty of the Hookah lingered in my mind, but the amazing revelation of Louisa and Jocoab made me uneasy. I had known them all my life. I didn't know what was true and what was false. I finally drifted into a light sleep. I was awakened by a loud, thunderous rumble. Chase sat up petrified. He held on to me and buried his face in my arms as bright flashes of light zigzagged around our room. With Chase clinging to me, I jumped out of the bed. I tried to persuade him to stay under the covers, but he held on to me and wouldn't let go. Momma and Helen came out of their room, hugging each other in fear. The four of us proceeded very cautiously toward the clamor. It kept getting louder and louder, rising to a din that pained my ears. Putrid smelling air wrapped around us like a burning blanket getting hotter and hotter as we neared the kitchen door.

"It burns my nose to breathe," Helen wheezed as she pulled on my nightshirt and tried to hold us back. "The house is on fire," she screamed. "We're gonna get burned."

"We're not gonna get burned. You and Chase go back and climb out the bedroom window. Hurry and get out of here."

"I ain't going, Cyrus. I'm scared," Chase sobbed. His grip tightened.

Momma pried his arms from around my waist. "You and Helen follow me out the back. Turn around and look. See? There's no fire there."

They obeyed and went with Momma out around the back. Something seemed very odd to me. There wasn't any smoke at all. If there was a fire why wasn't there any smoke? And the heat was intense only near the kitchen doorway. Suddenly, the thunderous noise stopped and a chilling wind hit me from behind. The brightness died and left me standing in a darkened hallway. I heard Momma knocking on the front door. I went into the kitchen and pulled the overhead light chain. The room lit up. The table was up against the wall. I walked over and unlatched the door and let in my trembling family. We looked all about the room for flames or any embers and traces of fire. But there were none. After we were satisfied there was no danger, we all went into Momma's bed and stayed until sunup.

That morning, Momma gave me the responsibility of finding a new place to live. She depended on me. My sister and brother also looked to me to be there for them. I realized, for the first time, how much they depended on me.

When Chakka came by the grocery store later that afternoon, I told him we could no longer stay in Louisa's house. He begged me not to do anything until I talked to his mother.

"Why should I talk to your mother? It's my mother I'm worried about. Since my father died, my mother's very sad. If we keep living in that house, she'll go crazy. My brother is so scared he won't go into any room unless someone's with him. This could make Helen nervous for the rest of her life."

"My mama know. She tell you what you don' know. She tell you 'bout Cybella."

"Cybella? What the hell are you talking about?"

"You come tonight. Mama tell you all. Please, you must come."

After work, I found Verolga, as usual, sitting on the porch with the Hookah.

"Allo, boy. You want smoke?"

"Not now, Madame Verolga."

She motioned for me to sit on a rug that was waiting for me.

"Chakka said you know things I don't know but should know. Can you help me find out why these things are happening to us?"

"Why you move here?"

"Because Louisa let my mother have the rooms for almost nothing. She and Jocoab wanted to help us. "

"No. That no why you get to live in Circus House. Circus House only for circus people."

"Oh, now I get it. You people are playing some kind of trick on us to get us to move out because we're not circus people. Well, you're doing a good job. We're moving."

"No, boy. Nobody play trick on you. All people here want you stay. You circus people."

"How many times I gotta tell you, we ain't circus people."

"Chakka!" she called her son. "Come out. Tell him."

Chakka stood in the doorway. "You circus people. Mama tell you now 'bout Cybella."

Bewildered by these two strange people from who knows where, I gazed at the dancing flowers in the Hookah and swore I was being put under their hypnotic spell.

Chakka came and sat next to me. "Smoke." He handed me a Narbeesh.

74

"No, Chakka. You're trying to pull something off on me." I put the Narbeesh down. "I gotta keep a clear head."

The old woman slowly began her story. "Cybella very beautiful gypsy dancing girl. Come from Egypt. She dance in Europa, Russia, all over with circus. Circus go back to Africa and is no more. Cybella stolen and sold to slave shippers. Young man, your gran'father' father, see her and want love her. He buy her for his pleasure. But he love her so strong that he take her home to America. He make her wife. Cybella want dance circus again. Love for Cybella make him circus man. They have baby, your father."

"Chakka, what kind of nonsense is she telling me? This has nothing to do with me. My name is Cyrus Allyrdice. My mother is English and my father was American. His father was Irish. His mother, I know, came from Sicily."

"No. She come from Egypt in Africa. He tell every body she come from Sicily. Your father he tell you 'bout his father? How he die?"

"He died in a fire when my father was a boy."

"He die hanging from rope. Right here where you live."

"My grandfather didn't die hanging."

"Do not get 'cited. I mean no harm. I respect good man. He circus man. Buy circus, let Cybella dance. We waiting for you for long, long time. Wait for you to grow to man. Wait to get you to Circus House." Chakka offered me the Narbeesh again.

"Who waited for me? For what? I don't believe any of this crazy stuff." Anger against the old lady, Chakka, and the whole tenement community was boiling inside me.

"Please, boy, calm. Here, smoke. I no do harm. When he come here with Cybella, she sick with heart. Not good. They live in what you call car'van wagon on this, his father' land. There is barn where Circus House now is. You know his name? Cyrus, like you."

"I know. I was named after him." I was gruff when I answered her.

"Listen to Verolga. Then you go see Louisa and Jocoab. Ask why they want you live Circus House."

As he spoke, I remembered, as a young boy, hearing my father speaking a very unusual foreign language with Louisa and Jocoab. They always stopped when they saw me.

"You must help you gran'father. I tol' you everything I see in crystal. When you father's father die. He very brave man."

"People see him with dark woman he say his wife. See her with baby. Blue eyes, like him, and black hair curly like dark skin Mama. They tell him woman must go from this, his home. He tell them get off his land. His woman stay. He stay."

"Tell me something. Are Louisa and Jocoab any relation to me?"

"She you father sister."

I was stunned by that shocking revelation; however, she went on as though I had no reaction or feelings about what they knew and were saying about the Allyrdice family.

"When Cyrus say no, people say he can no live this place if he keep Cybella wife. They want him go 'way." The old woman's voice was raspy and fading. She called for Nardelia to bring tea. "Chakka, tell boy. You know, same as me." She released the crystal and dabbed her moist face and hands with the hem of her dress.

"You father never tell you Louisa you aunt?" Chakka asked.

"He never did and neither did Louisa. Is she going to let us in on the secret now?"

"I no know what Louisa going tell you. 'Special you. She need you help. Circus people here need you help."

"You keep hinting that I can do something to save circus people. Why don't you explain to me exactly what it is that you want me to do."

"Is not easy thing we ask you do. First, I must tell sad story of Cyrus and Cybella."

The old woman put her fingers to her lips and kissed them. Then she placed her hand on my head and let her hand slide down my cheek and under my chin. "You have face of innocent man child. You must be strong like man tonight. Tomorrow you be child no more. You be man." She withdrew her hand and let Chakka tell me about my heritage.

"One night, men come from town. They have torch and gun. Cyrus in barn where Circus House now. Cybella and boy, you father, and baby Louisa in wagon house. These bad evil men go in take Cybella. She fight hard to save babies but she die in fight. Cyrus run out of barn. He see men with torch and gun. His wife dead on ground. He go crazy. He has ax. He swing and kill maybe two. But many mens fight him. They knock him down. Beat him. Then they take him in barn and hang him up on rope. Other mens carry Cybella body in barn and lay her down by where Cyrus hang. They put torch to hay and burn barn. Cyrus and Cybella are no more."

I felt a helplessness, listening to Chakka, and yet, a rage boiled deep down in the pit of my being, fighting to free itself and burst out to help Cybella and Old Cyrus. My grandfather's strength became my strength. I knew who I was and where I came from. I understood Circus House.

Nardelia came out with three silver goblets of mate' and three long spoons on a tray. I needed time to come back to the present. I welcomed the quiet. Nardelia served the goblets to us. I noticed the spoon handles were made like straws.

"You like mate'?" Madame Verolga asked.

"I don't know. I never had it. What is it?"

"It is tea. I find in Brazil. Very good for boy now."

"She mean mate' calm you, make you relax. You have bad time now when we tell you of Old Cyrus and Cybella. You no want to believe but I think you know. Is true."

"You're right when you said I had a bad time. I don't think I can put into words the feelings I went through."

"We see you face," Nardelia said in her soft whispery voice.

I looked upon Nardelia's face for the first time. I was ashamed of myself that I was unkind to her before.

"Do not drink mate′ from chalice," she instructed. "Sip up bombilla. You call it 'straw.' You will like."

Louisa, Chakka told me, was found after the murders, wandering around the campsite by one of the circus roustabouts and given to Jocoab's parents to take care of. My father ambled around the area until he was found and brought to my great-grandfather. Great-grandfather spent more than ten years looking for Louisa, but when he found her, she was too attached to her circus family and he had grown too old to cope with the situation. So Louisa remained with the circus family, growing up to marry Jocoab. My father and Louisa wrote to each other and met whenever they could.

"You go see Louisa. She tell you what you must do. All circus people wait for you. I say no more. You go home now." Madame Verolga dismissed me.

I returned to the gray house they call Circus House. After dinner, I told my mother I was going upstairs to talk to Jocoab on some man-to-man subject. I had to think of some plausible explanation to discourage her from coming up later to spend some time visiting with Louisa.

"I understand." There were tears in her eyes. "If only your father were alive for you."

Louisa met me at the door and ushered me into the parlor where Jocoab was sitting with his growler of beer.

"Do you drink beer, Cyrus, or would you like a cream soda?"

"Nothing. I think you know why I'm here. Chakka and Madame Verolga told me that I must talk to you. Why didn't you tell me that you were my father's sister and my aunt?"

Louisa lowered her head before she spoke. "I had to wait for the time to be right. I asked Madame Verolga and Chakka to help me when the time came to tell you about my father and mother, because Madame Verolga is very old and remembers details that I know nothing about. I will tell you what I remember, especially about your father."

"Don't be too hard on your aunt, Cyrus," Jocoab said. "She's lived through years of nightmares waiting for you."

"Why is everyone saying they've been waiting for me? My only concern is my mother, sister and brother. We're scared to death living in your house. We haven't got a peaceful night's sleep in the few days we've been here."

"We know that, son." Louisa was sympathetic. "But you're the only one who can ease the pain of what was done. You're the only one who can rectify the ending of that horrible deed and help Cyrus and Cybella in their eternal rest."

"I'm only a fifteen-year-old boy and you want me to rectify something that happened long before I was born? I can't even find peace in the here and now for my own family?"

"I know what you've been going through every night since you came here. Please listen and don't misunderstand or take what I'm going to say as some kind of a joke or idea of some crazy circus people. Please be patient with me. It's not easy for me to tell you. I pray you will hear us out and not turn and leave. Believe me when I say everything depends on your loyalty to our family. Past and present. I would like you to promise me that someday, when Chase and Helen are at an understanding age, you'll tell them about Cyrus and Cybella.'

"I promise, Aunt Louisa."

She pressed me into her immense bosom and kissed me. "Please tell them how much Jocoab and I love them."

Louisa and Jocoab unraveled a plan so bizarre it would involve superhuman effort to perform. They told me my grandfather spoke to Madame Verolga while she was in one of her trances. He told her to have Louisa find me and to get me into Circus House. Once I came to know about him and my father and Cybella, he would show me the way to them.

"Don't be afraid, Cyrus. Your grandfather will be there for you," Louisa assured me.

Jocoab took a few quick sips from his growler, wiped his mustache with the back of his hand and seemed to search his mind to find the right words. "The table has been moving around the room since the first night the other tenants moved in. Madame Verolga told Louisa that was the first announcement of your Grandfather's presence. Your grandfather told Madame Verolga that you, being the oldest living male member of his bloodline, had to be called upon to help him. He needed you."

"So since I was chosen, you people very cleverly manipulated us to moving into your haunted house. Right?"

"Because we are desperate."

"My mother's completely unaware of Louisa's true identity and my father's family background. Or for that matter, her children's true heritage."

"Yes, that's true. Don't hate us for that."

"Will you help us?" Louisa tearfully asked.

"I have no other choice."

We decided to put the plan in operation the following night, when Momma would be staying over at her place of employment. She was at ease, thinking Helen and Chase would have a restful night sleeping upstairs at Louisa's. But Louisa and Jocoab had taken them elsewhere for the night. I was afraid, I'll admit. Afraid to go through with the plan and afraid not to. When everyone left, I walked through the house and checked the rooms. For what, I don't know. I closed every door and put out the lights and pulled down all the shades. I sat alone in total darkness. To calm my trembling, I took deep breaths and exhaled cautiously and silently.

Chakka came over to spend the early hours with me. Chakka was older than I. Perhaps he was close to thirty, I don't know. I liked him because he treated me as an equal. I never had a friend like him before. We sat in that tomblike atmosphere for a long, long time.

"Open shade and let bright moon light room, so I let you see what I brought for you take on journey."

I raised a shade and the moonlight rushed around the room. I sat back down on the floor next to my friend.

"I want you have this." Chakka handed me a pearl handled knife. "It is very old, but good. Can do many things with knife."

"I can't take it. Looks like you spent a lot of money on that."

"No. It was give me by good circus man, Old Cyrus, when I small boy. I want you keep." He got up and walked to the door. "My Mama say, 'Tell boy I say gypsy prayer for him.' I say, 'My friend no boy. Is very brave man. Very, very brave man.'" He opened the door and walked out into a starry night.

I had a feeling we would never see each other again.

It was way after midnight when I heard the rumble sound far off in the distance. I recognized it immediately as the sound that has been haunting me since I came to this house, the sound of rolling wagon wheels mixed with the hard pounding of horses' hoofs. It got louder and louder as it came closer to Circus House. The ground under me shook and the house moved from its foundation. Momma's newly acquired oak table slowly rolled across the room. Shivers traveled down my back and I could feel the beads of sweat forming on my scalp and forehead. My underarms were damp and sticky. I raised myself up off the floor to the height of the windowsill and looked out to see a house-wagon surrounded by an unruly bunch of white-robed men holding burning torches. One of them broke from the mob and ran up the steps leading to the door of the house-wagon. Two more white robes rushed up to help him bash down the door. The three of them went into the house-wagon. I watched them carry out a woman dressed in nightclothes. It was Cybella. They dragged her down the steps and stood her up against the house-wagon.

"We told you to leave this place. Now you're gonna go for good, you and you're whole brood," they shouted. One hooded attacker ripped off her nightclothes. A small boy came down from the wagon and tearfully pushed through the scuffle to embraced Cybella around her knees. She reached down and touched his head then dropped to the ground.

My fear turned to anger. I wanted to run to help her and the child, but I was helpless. I couldn't hold back my tears. Suddenly, I loved Cybella. But it was different than the love I knew with my family. It felt deeper. I came to know passion as I watched someone I love die.

"She's dead." A shout went up. "The bitch is dead."

The boy, sobbing and gasping, threw himself upon his mother. One of the hooded mob distinguished himself by wrenching the boy away from the lifeless body. He held the child over his head, then threw him into the crowd. They played a game of toss with the boy who would grow up to become my father. When they tired of the game, someone flung him out toward the wooded area.

High in the sky, a shameful moon hid its face behind a drifting cloud, leaving the burning torches of the mob to create shadows among the shadows.

Cyrus came from out of those shadows, swinging his ax, felling anyone who dared to oppose him. He fought fiercely, making his way toward Cybella. When he reached Cybella, the night became silent again. The moon quietly sneaked out from its hiding place behind the cloud and let its silvery light shine on Cyrus and Cybella. For one brief calm moment, no one moved, no one made a sound. They watched the tall, bearded Cyrus take the woman in his arms and kiss her. The peace of the moment was shattered by the piercing explosion of a marksman's rifle. Cyrus and Cybella fell. I watched a little girl walk out of the house-wagon and down the steps. Pushing her way, she came to stand beside her fallen mother and father. It was Aunt Louisa.

The men of the mob began to pick up their dead and lay them in the carts. One of them yelled out, "Hey, what are we going to do with these two?"

"Check to see if they're dead. If not, make sure they are."

One of the rabble went over and kicked Cyrus. "Hey, this guy ain't dead yet."

"Leave him die right there," somebody answered.

"Oh, no!" a reply came back. "That son of a bitch killed three of ours. We ought to hang him."

"No tree strong enough in this clearing. Bring him in the barn and hang him there."

They picked up Cyrus and trampled over Cybella.

My skin was prickled and cold with terror as they turned and paraded toward me. Verolga told me that the foundation of Circus House was built where the barn was; I was in the barn. I didn't know if they could see me the way I saw them. I wanted to heave my guts out, but I was paralyzed with fear. I couldn't move a muscle.

They came into the barn, dragging my grandfather by his feet. They looked around for something to set him on. He was still alive. I prayed he would survive.

The livestock stirred in the stalls, nervously baying and barking. The dog bared his teeth and geared to attack.

"Shoot the damn dog and anything else that gets in the way," the leader commanded. The dog leaped and the blast of a well-aimed shotgun took him down. The chickens and other creatures were spared and dispersed. They found the worktable and moved it into the center of the barn under the main crossbeam. They set their victim on the worktable, trussed his arms and feet, then they made a hangman's noose and put it around his neck.

"Wait. Bring in his whore and let him gaze at her one last time."

Two of them went out and brought in Cybella. They placed her in front of the worktable, then hoisted my grandfather up, letting his toes dangle and inch from the worktable's surface. Two or three others set torches to the hay. When the flames began to threaten their safety, they ran out to watch the barn burn to the ground.

Flames leaped quickly and traveled from stall to rafters in a matter of seconds. I had very little time to complete what I was destined to do. I ran to the dangling form of my grandfather and climbed up on the worktable. I cut him down with Chukka's knife and laid him on the worktable. I jumped down and struggled to lower his still warm body to the dirt floor. The flames challenged my every move. I had to hurry and finish before the barn collapsed on us. I pushed the worktable out of the way. The reverberation of the table scrapping along the ground was the sound I heard in the kitchen of Circus House. I had no time to dwell on it. I ran over to Cybella. To my surprise, her body was also warm. I brought her over to her husband. I laid them side by side and put her hand in his.

My grandfather did not die in a hangman's noose. He died next to my grandmother. I know she waited for him to take her hand before she died. I know also that they knew me as their own, because they waited so long for me to come. I said good-bye and sadly left the burning pyre.

When I reached safety, I turned and looked about. The barn had disappeared. Circus House was there in its place. I looked over to the tenement for Chakka and Madame Verolga, but the building was deserted. All the apartments were boarded up. I knew they had gone forever. Helen and Chase came running towards me, bewildered that Louisa and Jocoab were nowhere to be seen. Chase saw the knife glistening in the sunlight. I handed Chukka's knife to my brother. "My best friend gave it to me. He got it from a circus man."

A warm zephyr swept past my face as we stood before our house. It wasn't like any other house I'd ever seen. It was painted a warm tone of gray. Our house exuded pride and dignity. It bid us a cheerful "Welcome home." My sister, Helen, entered the house first.

***

THE GEORGE RAFT SYNDROME

A jail cell with a no-seat toilet on the
isolation wing ain't no place for a musician like me.
I got a serial number and a security guard for a
doorman. It's for my own protection, because my
life is in danger. The worst part of this lousy life is
not being able pick up my horn and blow whenever
I want to.

How I got here is the kind of story they
write about in books. Come to think of it, it would
make one damn good movie. Who would they get to
play me? I've had plenty of time to dwell on that
subject. With my personality and classic good
looks, it wouldn't be easy. Just kidding.

Who would I suggest to play me? I could
see a defiant James Cagney gripping the bars of a
cell door and spitting in the "Turnkey's" face. Then
again, Cagney was rough on females. Squashing a
grapefruit in Mae Marsh's face. You gotta treat
women with kid gloves. Or maybe sallow-jowls
Humphrey Bogart, pacing the floor and making
escape plans. He's a little too wishy-washy. I
thought about the Birdman, Burt Lancaster. But not
for long. I guess the best of the lot, and that includes
Eastwood, is George Raft. Raft in prison grays,
gazing at a picture of Ann Sheridan, the 'Oomph
Girl'. Raft was a romantic. I could identify with
him. He'd do anything for a good-looking broad.

I enjoy women. I love them for their
mystery and sensual allure. Their very aura excites

me. And like Raft, I would do anything for a good-looking broad. Thereby hangs my fate.

I met my Ann Sheridan in Atlantic City, before they brought in the casinos. Her name? Shayna. Beautiful, voluptuous woman, whose fiery glance made promises and told lies all in one look. Large dark eyes that will haunt you until you lock your lids for the very last time.

Shayna and I worked at Skins Brasil's Crystal Room. All the big stars appeared there. But to those in the know, it was a hang out and pick-up joint for the Godfathers from the Garden, Empire and Quaker states and their trusted henchmen.

But I digress. I was reminiscing about Shayna. Shayna was a Bar Girl or 'B Girl' as they were better known. She was employed by Skins to be overly friendly with the male customers. Flatter them, you know, so they'd feel privileged to spend money on her watered-down drinks. When ordered by Skins Brasil, she'd take the customer to a hotel to spend the night. If I'm not mistaken, Skins owned the hotel too. But I may be speculating. Everybody in town knows Skins is just a front man.

I played first trumpet with the house orchestra. Usually, during the band's break time, I'd go out back in the alley and join the other musicians and show people out there for a drink or a smoke. Some guys had a flask or a bottle wrapped in a plain brown paper bag. And a 'joint' went from one set of lips to another. On the night it all came down, Glen, the tenor sax in the band, and I had finished a dance set. We went into the Lounge bar during the break. If Shayna and Rita Marie were free for the night, we

had plans to take them with us, to an after-hours
'Jam Session.' Rita Marie was Shayna's roommate.
She also worked as a B Girl out of Skins' stable.
My friend, Glen, had the hots for chubby little Rita
Marie.

While Glen and I sat with our drinks, talking
about music and musical arrangements, I saw Skins
come out of his office with Shayna and Rita Marie.
They made their way towards some crooked-nosed,
ugly guy sitting directly opposite me on the other
side of the wide oval bar. Shayna caught my eye
and winked. I raised my glass to her. Shades of
George Raft. Skins stayed only a moment to
introduce the girls to the creep. The guy finished his
drink, dropped a tip, and left with Shayna and Rita
Marie.

Break time was up, so Glen and I returned to
the main showroom to play until closing. Then we'd
make the after-hours club and blow until past
sunrise. I blew my heart out that night. All the great
ones were assembled at the club, Miles, Garner,
Sammy and Sarah, jamming and blowing. It was
inspirational. Then again, I guess you have to have
lived it.

While Glen was riffing, I leaned against the
bar surveying the scene. Through all the smoke and
perspiration, I sensed Shayna in the room. Her
perfume was as recognizable as her voice.
Suddenly, a warm jolt rushed through my body. I
felt two arms slide from behind my neck and caress
me. My skin prickled as her lips touched the back of
my neck. The hairs all over my body changed
position, from lay-down relaxed to military alert.

She breathed, "I'm in trouble, baby. I need your help. Meet me outside. I'll be in the blue Caddy around the corner." Before I could turn she was gone.

Shayna rolled down the window. Her face was ashen. She tried to act composed, but I could tell she was petrified. She tilted her head toward me. Those big soft brown eyes of hers sought mine.

"I'm glad you came, lover."

"You thought I wouldn't?"

She reached up and pulled my head through the rolled-down window and kissed my lips. I tasted the saltiness of her tears. Her tremor passed on to me. I felt the softness of her cheeks as I tried to brush away her tears.

"Baby, what's wrong? Tell me what's happened."

"I'm in deep, deep trouble. Very deep trouble."

"What the hell's up? Where'd you get the Caddy?"

From the passenger side, a quivering Rita Marie sobbed uncontrollably "It belongs to him. We stole it."

"Will somebody tell me what's going on? What does she mean, you stole it?"

"Borrowed it," Shayna turned and corrected Rita Marie. She reached for her purse on the floor and began searching through it for a Kleenex. "Is that all you can ask? Don't you get the message? She dabbed her eyes. "I killed Skins' friend."

"You what?"

"I killed the bastard you saw me with at the bar."

"You killed somebody?"

"Yeah, we killed somebody. Now quit saying that, and get it through your head, we are in quicksand."

"How? What happened? Did he hit you? What?"

"Don't you understand? We can't stay around here any longer. We've got to get away. Fast. Just help us. I'll tell you all about it when we're off the street."

"You're right. You're right. But I just got hit between the eyes. It's gonna take a minute to revive."

"What're we gonna do? Where we gonna go?" Rita Marie's pitiful sobs begged me for help.

"What the hell are you gonna do? You can't stay here in Atlantic City. We gotta get you to a safe place."

"There ain't no safe place. They'll find us."

"Rita Marie, stop crying and start thinking." Shayna tried to calm Rita Marie's fears; she also seemed to be talking to herself. "We're gonna be okay."

"Move over and let me drive." I opened the door. "I'm gonna take you to my place."

"No. First, I got to get rid of this car. I'm gonna drive it and park it somewhere near his hotel. You follow me. Then you can take us over to your place."

Shayna may have been frightened, but she was in control. That's what I admired in her: she was cool and gutsy. A woman like that stirs me up. I felt a rush. I followed Shayna as she drove up and down the Monopoly named streets of the city advertised as the 'Playground of the World.' She parked the car on a dark side street, within walking distance of the hotel. I pulled up alongside, expecting them to jump into my car. They kept me waiting for two or three minutes before they got in. "What the hell took you so long?"

"We wiped down the steering wheel and door handles. God forbid we should leave a fingerprint."

"I'm only gonna drive by my place and pull up in front so you two can get out. The key to the back door is under the loose brick on the first step. When you get inside, don't make too much noise. Play it quiet and down. We don't want to draw the neighbors' attention. I'm going back to get Glen. We'll be there in a little while."

"Now I'm really scared." Rita Marie never stopped blubbering and sniffling.

I wondered how I was going to explain to Glen that stashed away in my digs were a couple of murderers, Shayna and the love of his life, Rita Marie.

Shayna had the coffeepot brewing when Glen and I got back to my place. Glen was still in a state of shock. He sat on the bed and pulled Rita Marie down on his lap. He held her close and let her cry it out. We all sat in silence until Rita Marie ceased her hysterics. When she finally stopped and the room was quiet, I asked Shayna to go over her story again, in detail. More detail.

"Tell me again. Right from the beginning. I want to know what was said in Skins' office. This time don't leave anything out."

Rita Marie spoke up, still quivering. "Skins said he had this client who wanted two girls. This was some VIP from out of town. It was some kind of a special reward. It had to be kept on the QT. Skins said if everything went all right, we'd get a special bonus because he was paying. This guy did something spectacular; they wanted to make sure he had a good time.

"I was surprised Skins told us that much. Usually, he just tells who and where, and we go. But this time, he was emphatic about us treating this guy extra special. 'He did a big favor for some very good friends of mine.' Those were Skins' exact words. That's why I'm so scared." Rita Marie buried her face in Glen's chest.

"When we got to the hotel," Shayna continued, "that creep had some crazy weird plans. Well, I'm gonna tell you right up front, I don't go for any perverts. Ninety-nine percent of the time, I don't do anything on these so-called dates. I always carry some pulverized Downers."

"I do the same," Rita Marie said. "We just get the 'johns' to pass out. Then I tell them the next day how terrific they were. Nobody's the loser and I can get some sleep."

"That's a little trade secret the 'johns' don't know about, and you shouldn't be telling, Rita Marie." Shayna giggled.

"He was the ugliest man I ever met. He kept laughing all the time and saying, 'I done a good job.

I done good. A really fucking good job. I put him so far away not even God's gonna find him on Judgment Day.' When I asked him what he done so good, he shoved me. All he said was, 'If they look a million years, they ain't never gonna find the son of a bitch. Never. I done a good job.'" Rita Marie sniffled. "'What kinda crazy talk is that?' I asked him. He told me that I wasn't there to ask him questions, I was there to show him a good time, help him celebrate what he done."

Glen my friend, who never had a date unless it was blind, had his arm around Rita Marie, bar hustler and self-confessed murderer. Rita Marie and Glen made a very odd couple. He was like a kid away from home for the first time: the sordid ways of the world were just being exposed to him, and he was going to taste every free sample. Rita Marie was small plump and an appetizer of what the sordid world had to offer. On second thought, maybe I'm the odd ball.

"Rita Marie kept him busy at first, just playing records and dancing. I fixed the drinks. Seltzer and lemon, that's all he drank. That's what he had at the club. No hard stuff. I put the downers in the bottom of the glass and fizzed the seltzer bottle. Then I squeezed in the lemon. I made three seltzers; his was the only one with the lemon."

"And the downers," I reminded her.

"Yeah, them too. I gave him the drink while he was dancing. He chug-a-lugged it all down without coming up for air. I could never do that with seltzer. Then out of a clear blue sky he turned and threw the empty glass at Rita Marie. He missed her head by a hair. 'That's for asking too many fucking questions,' he yelled at her. I got mad and went over and pushed him. He said that's the way he likes to start a party, 'Get a girl's temper flaring.'

"He told me I asked too many questions anyway for a hired broad," Rita Marie broke in.

Shayna glanced over at Rita Marie, then continued. "Next, he took off his tie and flung it at my feet. Then he unbuttoned his shirt and took it off. He came over and shoved it my face. Now my temper flared like the Fourth of July. He loosened his belt and unzipped his fly letting his pants fall to the floor. He kicked them off over his shoes. I picked up his tie and shirt and wrapped them around his head. Rita Marie picked up his pants and went through the pockets. Somehow, he got the shirt off his head and he spied Rita Marie holding his wallet. He lunged at her and they both fell to the floor. He punched and slapped her, beating her."

Shayna opened her purse and took out a pack of Luckies. "I went to her. I grabbed the tie that was still around his neck. I tightened it. Hard as I could. I never let go."

Shayna paused again, broke the cellophane wrapper and took out a cigarette.

"I pulled it until he got on his hands and knees and crawled away from Rita Marie. He had the most scary look in his eyes. I didn't care."

I watched her put the cigarette to her lips. I took out my lighter and held the flame as she drew in.

"The bastard was slime," left her lips along with the cigarette smoke. I refilled her coffee cup.

Her slender fingers had ceased trembling. As I poured, I noticed that the nail of her left index finger had broken off, marring the pink symmetry of her manicure.

"I got on his back, but I never let go of the tie. I rode him like a horse and led him over to the bed. If he wanted kinkie, I'd give him just a little kinkie. But that's all he was gonna get. But the son of a bitch passed out on me."

"He just pooped out under her," Rita Marie added.

Shayna went on. "Rita Marie and I struggled to get him up on the bed. We turned down the blankets, then we lifted him up on the bed. After we got him on the bed, I got on it and removed the tie from around his neck. Rita Marie knelt down at the bedside and pushed him, while I tried to get him toward the middle. All of a sudden, he jolted up so fast I fell back. He sat up and grabbed at his chest."

Rita Marie interrupted. "He made a funny whimper, then fell to his side. He never moved again."

"That's right, he did make that funny noise. It sounded like a cry," Shayna continued. "Together, we struggled to straighten him out. He never moved a muscle. And I didn't hear his heavy breathing. It was then I was almost certain he must be dead. Those downers work fast, but not like that."

"That's when she told me to get the mirror out of my purse."

"I saw it done in a movie. I really didn't know what I was doing. I put it near his mouth and I

98

shook his head. Still no breath. I put my ear down on his chest; I couldn't hear his heart beat. He was dead. I killed him."

Shayna's composure amazed me. Without a shudder or a trace of remorse, she described in detail how she caused a man to die.

"You're telling me that you made it appear that he came home, undressed, switched out the light, got in bed and died in his sleep?"

"That's right. We had to do it that way. Next, we took off the rest of his clothes, socks and shorts. You know, to make it look like he did it himself."

"How do you know he slept in the raw when he was alone?" Glen wanted to know.

"I figured I've been around so many creeps like him, I know just how they are."

"Shayna fixed him up in the bed. She tucked him in, fixed the sheets. You know, to look normal like. After Shayna told me he was dead, I didn't want to touch him."

"No, you just went through all his pockets," I joked.

"He still had one shoe and sock on. Shayna took them off and placed both his shoes side by side, under the bed."

"You should have seen Rita Marie. She folded his underwear and socks. I hung up his shirt and pants. Even placed his tie over the back of the chair.

"You did it so nice and neat, Shayna. He had a 'cross and a crown of thorns' tattoo on his arm," Rita Marie sobbed.

"He was shit and a creep. But like I said, I could tell he was meticulous. Those kind always are. They did things to please their mothers. They were neat and tidy."

"You should write a book," Glen said, in all innocence.

"Maybe someday I will, when this blows over and all's forgotten."

"We knew we had to get hell out of there, fast." Rita Marie's bleached blond hair was matted and uncombed. Her cheek was bruised, and her mascara-blotched eyes stained Glen's shirt.

"We cleaned up the place: washed and dried the glasses and went around wiping up anything we thought we touched. We didn't want to leave one finger print."

"What did you take? Jewels? Credit cards? Nothing that can be traced to you, I hope."

"Only money. I swear nothing else. We weren't stickin' around with a corpse watchin' us. His eyes were open wide." Rita Marie squeezed her eyes closed and shivered her shoulders.

"We just took our pay."

"The pay was good. We deserved it." Shayna's tone implied resentment to the deceased for permitting them to murder him.

"And a little bonus, I presume."

"You had to get that little dig in, you son of a bitch." Shayna smiled sardonically.

"What happens now?" Glen asked.

"I don't know. But I think the girls have got to get out of town. Pronto."

"How and where?"

"For now, you have got to lay low. We gotta come up with a plan." I took Shayna's hands in mine. "Did you tell anyone else about this?"

"No. The only thing we did before I came to you was to go over to our place and pack our bags. We knew we'd had it in this town. You were the only trustworthy one I could think of." Shayna put her arms around me. Every time she touches me, I have the same physical reaction: I turn into mush. Like George Raft, I talk strong and carry a soft heart. "You guys try to get some sleep. Meanwhile, I'll take a walk over by the hotel, see what I can see or hear."

"Please be careful." Shayna kissed me.

The sun was already high in the sky when I got to the Hotel Thor's back service entrance... just in time to see the morgue attendants loading the body into the hearse.

"What the hell you doing here?" Jimmy Dugan, the cop on duty, asked. He knew me from coming into the club and for a couple of other things related to his line of work.

"Oh, just on my way to get the papers and do a few errands. What happened here?"

"Some out-of-town gangster was found dead."

"Murdered?"

"They ain't sure. However, they know who he is and the game he plays. Between you and me, he's a hit man. Got a rap sheet a mile long. Big question is, what the hell was he doin' in our town"

"Could be he was just getting a little R and R."

"That ain't funny."

"Didn't mean it to be. This is a resort town."

"It looks—on the surface, mind you—like he died of a heart attack. The coroner will know for sure after the autopsy."

"Heart attack? Don't those guys die the way they live? Guns and knives?"

"Naw, nothing like that here. It coulda been worse though. It coulda been done hit style. But for now, the investigation is just routine. We know he had a lady of the evening with him.

"How the hell do they know that?"

"They found a piece of a woman's fingernail on the bed sheets. Painted pink, it was. Odd thing, they didn't find any fingerprints. It's the fingernail that the mystery hangs on. The broad was probably too much for him and he just keeled over. I guess she got the hell scared outta her and took off."

"I saw all the commotion and thought it was just some drunk fallen down or an accident. But murder! Don't look too good for tourist trade."

"Well, you can say it was a robbery too: she cleaned him out. They didn't find one red cent in cash in the room. You know, if I was the broad that was with him, I'd be on my way to Canada or some other foreign country."

"Why? If it was a heart attack, she's got nothing to fear."

"She's got a hell of a lot to fear, because this guy is famous for his talents as a hit man. He was here for a reason. The boys down at the station house are happy to see him rest in peace; not so with those guys with the crooked noses. They're gonna wanna know if he did a little pillow talking before his final breath, so they ain't never gonna stop looking for that gal. And if she was one of Skins' broads, he's got her marked. God help her if Skins gets her first. She's done for. It so happens that they don't call him Skins because he's skinny. That guy will rip the skin of anybody's bones what fucks with him."

"It's as big as that, huh?"

"This ain't the family vacation place it used to be."

"You can say that again."

"You work down at Skins' joint, don't you? Some kind of musician, right?"

"Yes, and that's all I am. And if I ever so much as looked at one of his broads, he'd have me circumcised all over again. Skins don't confide in me." I wanted to say 'like you do.' I know Jimmy Dugan slightly. I don't know why he let me in on some of the details of the murder. The only explanation I come up with is Jimmy Dugan likes to make himself important. He wanted me to know he was on a mob job.

"Well, I guess those boys got their rules and regulations like the rest of us."

"That's right. No lookie and no nookie."

Jimmy Dugan laughed and waved his baton. "Get the hell out of here before I run ya in."

"Well, I guess I'll get the papers and go on home. See ya around, Jim."

"Hey, the papers are already running the story," Jimmy called to me. "Some eager-assed local reporter got a scoop on this thing."

I got in my car, closed my eyes and rested my head against the raised headrest and just caved in.

"Jesus God, they're in one helluva a mess."

"Did you see Skins?" Shayna asked as I came through the door. It was obvious Shayna was more frightened of Skins than the police.

"No I didn't see Skins."

"You took so long, I thought maybe you went by the club."

"I went down to the hotel and talked to a cop I know." I handed the newspaper to Glen.

Glenn glanced at the headlines. "The cops found him already, huh?" He flung the paper on the bed.

"Yeah. It's all there in the paper. Evidently, this guy had an early appointment with one of his cohorts. When they got no answer from his room, they got the manager."

"So I guess Skins knows. He'll be wanting to hear from me and Rita Marie."

"I guess so."

"Oh, no! I ain't gonna go and see Skins. He'll kill us." Rita Marie began to shake violently.

"Don't worry, Ree. We'll find a way out." Glen went to her and held her in his arms.

"So what did the cop say?" Shayna asked.

"They're not sure how he died. The cop said they think he died of a heart attack. The coroner hasn't performed an autopsy yet."

"They'll find out."

"Shayna, have you told me everything? You sure you didn't leave anything out?

"Whaddya mean?"

"You told me where it happened, how it happened and why. But you never told me his name."

"Look, Skins said his name was Tonto or Toronto, something like that."

I could tell Shayna was getting tense.

"I didn't care what his name was."

"Do you know his real name? You must've found out his name when you went through his wallet and took all his dough. Didn't you read his drivers license?"

"Yeah," Rita Marie's sorrowful, brown eyes filled with tears again. "I don't remember too good. It was Alfonso something or other. It was a big long name that starts with a gee."

"Did you find out if the cops know his name?" Glen asked.

"Yes, the cops know his name. His address. And his occupation. He plays on the bad guys' side. He ain't no Tonto. He's a hit man from out of state. You girls—and I guess, us guys—are in deep, deep shit. The paper didn't mention his name, but it says that the FBI is getting involved."

"What the hell's the FBI want? The cops put it down as a heart attack, right?" Glen said weakly.

"Oh, if it's a heart attack, then we're safe, Shayna." Rita Marie heaved a sigh of relief.

"It's not so easy as that, Rita Marie. They're gonna do an autopsy. Then they're gonna see all the downers and the seltzer mixed in his stomach or kidneys or whatever."

"He coulda taken those himself."

"Yeah, he took the downers with the seltzer from a glass with no finger prints. They got enough to work with those clueless clues," I threw to Rita Marie. She began to cry again.

"But if he did die of natural causes, they won't be looking for no murder or murderer," Glen tried to rationalize to ease Rita Marie's fears.

"Then we don't have to be afraid?" Rita Marie almost pleaded.

I didn't want them to panic, so I explained as simply and as emphatically as I could. "The cops know that Tonto had a babe in his bed sometime before, after or during, his death scene. And they are not about to forget that."

"How do they know? We were very careful to clean up everything."

I took Shayna's hand and kissed her fingertips. "Are you aware that you broke your nail?"

"I hate when that happens."

"The police found the broken piece between the sheets. They like the color pink you use. That's how they know he was with a babe."

"Can they trace me from that?"

"I don't know, baby. You gotta remember, it only ain't the police and the FBI we got to worry about, it's Skins' friends."

"If Skins is looking for us, there ain't nowhere in the world to hide. My God, what're we gonna do, Shayna?"

Glen tightened his arms around Rita Marie and held her close to his chest. "Please, Rita Marie,

I'll help you. Skins or nobody else is going to hurt you."

"Between J. Edgar Hoover and Skins Brasil, some hell of a spot to be in. You're right, Rita Marie. We gotta find somewhere off the planet to hide."

"I gotta be with you, Shayna. We gotta stay together."

"I think you'd be safer if we split, Rita Marie. I might go in a commune out west or meet up with the fleet in Galveston. We gotta fend for ourselves now. The first part is not where, but how. How are we gonna get out of Jersey, let alone Atlantic City?"

"The one thing in your favor is that they won't be looking for two girls. They're only interested in one. The one with the broken pink finger nail."

"You sure know how to make a working girl's day, lover." Shayna stretcher her arms and spread her fingers. We all stopped and looked as she held them out before us. "If it weren't so serious, I'd laugh and recite that song we used to sing about the ten little Indians."

"And then there were nine," Glen chimed in.

"Damn, now I gotta file them all down and change the color. Rita Marie is a cosmetologist and manicurist. She'll take care of my fingernails. You're right about Skins though. I've known him to do some cruel things when he's crossed."

"I've got an idea, but you gotta stay together for a little while." I didn't want to get their hopes up too high. "It might work."

"I don't know about you, Shayna, but I swear on my mother's grave that this is the end for me. I'm gonna get a real job. I'm going back to being a beautician."

"What're you gonna do with the money?" I asked them.

"I told you, we earned it. It's the beginning of the future. That's the way it is, period." Shayna was definite on the matter.

"We really did earn it the hard way," Rita Marie said.

"Okay, pal. What's your plan?" Glenn asked me.

"I think Skins kind of suspects that Shayna and I are friendly. At least, I know he's seen us talking in the club on a couple of occasions. But that's all. So I gotta go back to the club and stay till the end of my contract with the band. However, Glen hasn't got a contract, so he's gonna call his sister and tell her he wants to come home. But you just can't walk out on your job, so she's gonna wire you to come home. There's a death in the family. Think you can arrange that, Glen?"

Glen was over-anxious to comply. "I'll call her now."

"Glen, on second thought, maybe you should forget about it. Just go home alone. I'll get them out of here. It was wrong to get you involved in this."

"He's right, Glen," Shayna said. "If things go wrong, you could end up in jail. Or even worse, get killed. And that goes for you too." Shayna grabbed my arm and looked deep in my eyes. "You both better give this a second thought. I didn't think it would lead to this."

"I can't leave you and Rita Marie just like that," Glen insisted. "I'm staying."

"You heard the man. He speaks for me also."

"I don't want you guys to put your lives on the line for me. What about you, Rita?"

"I'd feel safer if Glen stayed with us."

"It's gonna work out. We'll be okay. You two are gonna make it out of here. I got a plan all worked out in my mind. But for now, you two gotta stay here until Glen gets back. He's got to talk to Skins and Al, the conductor, about going home."

"Before I go, tell me the rest of your plan," Glen said.

"Okay. You all got a right to hear. Maybe you got a better idea. Here's how it should work. When Glen comes back, he's gonna hide you in the back of his car, cover you over with blankets or something. I'd say one of you get in the trunk, but that may not be necessary. Then he'll drive you up to my sister's place. She married a farmer, and they have this dairy farm in Schohaire, upstate New York. She's got plenty of room. You could stay there until you decide what to do or until I get up there in three months."

"That's a terrific idea. It's a great place. You'll love it up there. I'll take the back road. We'll cut across Jersey to Pennsylvania, then up to Schoharie." Glen had been to the farm with me a couple of times.

"Will your sister and her husband like the idea?" Shayna didn't seem too keen for the farm.

"They're crazy about me. You worry too much. Clouds your thinking and motor skills."

"I'm going out to get the tank filled with gas now," Glen interjected.

"And I'm going out to call my sister. I think it best to use a pay phone. Thank God, we got a couple of good sisters." Glen looked out and checked up and down the street before he went out.

"You'll be safe in Schohaire. I'll get you out of this burg. Don't worry. It's all settled.

"I got no other choice. Skins knows, and when the cops start looking, they're gonna find me missing."

"Shayna, maybe we can go back to our place and pick up some more things."

"Oh, no, forget it. You are not to go over to your place. You got your pay to start you a new life."

Glen and the girls were gone when I got home from work that night, but the scent of Shayna lingered on. A woman is not just lipstick and nail polish. She is an atmosphere. A planet. A universe. Once a woman touches your life, she never leaves you. She may walk out on you, but when she does, she bequeaths you the memory of her movements as she saunters away. I lay down on the bed and lit a cigarette. I inhaled deeply and closed my eyes. I saw Shayna's face before me. I reached out to feel her soft skin. Her red full lips brushed mine. Her lips parted, and in my fantasy, I took her. No man could resist wanting to take her and hold her and smother her with himself. And yet no man could really have Shayna. She never fully gave herself. Shayna was desire personified. And desire is what it's all about. It's what drives us. Shayna knows how to keep a guy trailing along, but never alongside. Still, she is the one woman who has woven herself into my psyche, and I can't let her go.

The cigarette's ashes fell on my chest; the burn woke me from my reverie. As I brushed the ashes away, I noticed that the newspaper was still on the bed where Glen had left it. The top headlines were big and bold, about the murder at the hotel. It was a smaller second caption that caught my eye. It wasn't as played up as the Atlantic City story, just a blip that some union boss named Hoffa had been missing, FBI suspects foul play, and that it could be mob connected. I read a few lines about a tie-in with organized crime. That's when it hit me. I remembered Rita Marie telling us that the john kept bragging that he did such a good job, nobody would ever find him. Find who? The union boss?

While I was mulling these threads of inside information over in my mind, Jimmy Dugan knocked on my door.

Jimmy Dugan, in his own simple way, informed me, "It's just a technicality. We're rounding up all the hoodlums and bums for questioning. But for one very obvious reason, you just seem to stick out."

He and a couple of detectives put the cuffs on me and herded me off to the proverbial "downtown" for questioning. They were curious to know why I was at the back of the hotel on the morning the body was discovered. They worked hard to get me to implicate myself. But I stalled. I figured as long as they were talking to me, Glen and the girls were getting farther and farther away from the Jersey shore.

See, I knew from my encounter with Jimmy Dugan at the hotel that the creep died of natural causes. When I reminded them of that fact, they told me that they had a piece of fingernail with a particular shade of pink.

"I knew that too. Jimmy told me that," was my reply to their inquisition.

Jimmy Dugan winced. He knew he talked too much, and it made him look bad to his superiors.

"You know too much. That intrigues me," the chief of the interrogation responded. "I think you know more than what Officer Dugan informed you of."

Jimmy Dugan's wince turned to an expression of self-inflicted pain.

"We have here an autopsy report. Perhaps you're so well informed that you'd be willing to share your information with us."

It's all over. They found the downers I thought.

"Hey, I was just out to get the papers. What the hell has a broken finger nail, a dead body and downers have to do with me."

Suddenly, I heard a silence as loud as the atomic bomb. I saw their eyes glancing from one to the other. There were two of them besides Officer

Jimmy Dugan. One guy was thin and balding with pale white pasty skin. He asked me questions in a quiet polite kind of way. The other guy was heavy, kind of burly and sloppy, kept a cup of coffee in one hand and a cigarette in the other. When I dropped the bomb about the downers, he sputtered and spewed, drooling a mouthful of coffee down the front of his shirt.

I didn't know whether to shit or go blind. I knew I blew it. They went back to my place and brought their fine-tooth combs with them. And lo and behold, in a wastebasket, they found cotton balls, damp, with a trace of "Misty Pink" nail polish residue. Put that together with the broken fingernail and the broad or broads that the creep allegedly had in the room, and they come up with me. I tried to tell them that some one-night stand left me a little something to remember her by. They wouldn't buy it.

"That 'Misty Pink' nail polish matches the broken piece of nail we found," the blabbermouth Jimmy Dugan kept reminding me.

"You guys are all wrong. What do I know about Skins' connections and mobsters? Music is what I know. I play a trumpet. That's all."

"And where do you play?"

"At Skins Brasil's."

"That's the crux of the matter. At Skins Brasil's. Somehow you and Skins and one of his broads connect with this mob guy. You gotta remember, pal, Skins got the money and the control of this town, so it looks like you're 'it'... unless you can come up with the broad or broads, whatever the case may be. Another thing, you better start thinking of taking up light housekeeping with a member of the your own gender, in a room with no view."

"Jimmy, I ain't lying. I don't know anything about the creep. And I don't know anything about Skins or his broads."

"We told you, we ain't gonna prosecute the dame. He died of natural causes, as I said, so there's no Murder One. Our guys are worried for her safety. We do got a few questions we'd like to get answered before the mob finds her."

Things didn't work out like I planned. It seems the girls never got to Schohaire. Glen told me they left him at a road stop. They got in an eighteen-wheeler with a couple of guys. He couldn't stop them. Glen was too scared to come back to Atlantic City, so he's up in Jersey somewhere, in business with his father selling aluminum siding. And here I stay.

They're keeping me here in jail on a lot of little charges, plus a load of unpaid parking tickets. The press and the newscasts are turning me into a celebrity afraid for his life. Because the law's got me by one arm and the mob by the other, I got no future one way or the other.

What difference does it make today? They're all gone: Cagney, Bogart, Raft, Ann Sheridan, Shayna, Rita Marie, and even my friend, Glen. Somewhere out there, in some small run-down jazz joint, sitting on some dilapidated bar stool, there's a good-looking broad who'll throw back her head and dare you not to enjoy her laughter. She'll surround you with a perfumed scent that drives you up a wall. And maybe some lonely night, you'll see her smile and hear her laugh as her shadow eludes your grasp. If she winks, do me a favor, just raise your glass the way George Raft would and remember me to Shayna.

***

ACROSS THE DOUBLE YELLOW

Nick felt secure and comfortable in the squad car, especially with Harp at the wheel. But tonight he sensed a coolness in Harp's attitude that was never there before.

"Damn!" he blurted, "I just burned my lips. Why they make the coffee so freakin' hot, I'll never know. Gotta wait so freakin' long for it to cool off."

Harp never acknowledged or answered Nick's remark. He concentrated on driving, letting his eyes sweep over the area, from side to side and down the highway, a dexterity cops acquire after years of surveillance duty.

"Jeez, Harp, you're distant tonight. Whatsa matter, couldn't get it up last night?"

"Where is it written in the rule books that just because we share the ride, we gotta talk to each other?" Harp never turned his head as he spoke to his partner. He just kept his eyes peeled to the road, staying close to the double-yellow lines of the highway.

"Ain't no rule. Jeez, Harpy boy. Touchy tonight, ain't we?" Nick blew on his coffee. "It ain't never gonna cool down. Maybe I shoulda got another doughnut."

"You ate the first one so damned fast, I thought you'd choke. And you're such a slob. Look at you. Powdered sugar all down the front of your uniform. Disgraceful."

"Oh, shit, another cleaning bill." Nick furiously tried to brush the stain away. "That's because the coffee is too damn hot."

"Handle hot things and get burned fingers, I always say."

"Ain't you ever been burned by something hot?"

"Oh, I've poked around some hot coals in my time."

"Yeah. Like Errol Flynn, you kept your socks on."

"Nicky baby, you're quite perspicacious tonight."

"I'm what?"

"Look it up," Harp muttered out of the side of his mouth. "Not too much traffic tonight. Might as well make a U turn and head back."

Nick blew on his steaming coffee again. "County line is just up ahead."

"Wait a minute. Look what's this coming down the pike, on my side, across the double yellow lines."

"Looks like someone hailing us. By all appearances, I'd say, it's a woman."

"As I said, you surely are the astute one."

"There you go again with the big words."

Harp crossed over the double yellow, eased up alongside the walker and rolled down the window.

"Good evening, ma'am. Kinda dangerous, walking alone along the highway, especially at night."

Harp surveyed the trembling woman, completely, from the deep plunging cleavage beneath an expensive cashmere sweater, then wandered down to its roots. His eyes caressed her full, round breasts, while perceiving the bruises on her beautiful young face. They noticed her torn, ripped skirt spotted with mud and grass. But furtively lingered on the on the softness of her alluring breasts. Within a nanosecond, his proficient eyes surveyed the obvious. Then for a moment, he closed his eyes as he covertly envisioned the woman devoid of the obvious as she stood before him. The imagined vision of her soft skin covering taut, firm breasts aroused him. He could feel them pressing against his face.

"Car break down somewhere?" he heard himself ask.

"I went off the road about a mile back. I remember hitting my head against the top of the car before things went black. But I think I'm okay. Can you take me back there? I lost my purse. I couldn't find it when I left."

"What's your name?"

"Sara Farland. My license and ID are in my purse."

"Want us to call an ambulance?" Nick asked.

"I got a little shook up for a minute and I'm a little fuzzy. "I'll be all right, if I could just sit down.

"You'd better take a seat in the back." Harp got out and caressingly put his arms around her as he guided her into the car.

"Want me to radio it in, Harp?"

"Naw, we'll go up to the scene of the accident. She wants to get her purse. Then we'll call it in."

They drove slowly along the shoulder until they saw the tire tracks leading over the embankment and down into the gully. Harp parked the car and got out. "You can stay in the car, Nick. I'll take her out to look around."

"I can get out and help."

"It'll give you a chance to finish your coffee. It's probably cool enough by now, so you shouldn't burn yourself. When you finish the coffee, put up the road flashes if you think it necessary.

"Okay." Nick obliged his partner.

Harp opened the back door and helped Sara out of the car.

"Is Harp your last name?"

"No. It's a nickname. I come from an Irish father and a Mexican mother. I look typically Irish, so the family calls me Harp. My brother is very Latino looking, so they call him Chico."

"What an amusing story." Sara walked in front of Harp as they made their way into the gully.

"Yeah, every time I tell it, the ladies get a charge out of it."

"Are there many ladies?"

Harp ignored the question.

"I think you'd better let me go ahead of you. I have the flash. You know, there's a lake just beyond that clump of trees. It's a good thing your car got stuck in this soft mud or you might have hit the trees and landed in the lake."

"Don't tell me that. I'm still shaky."

The Mercedes was poised at a precarious angle. The front bumper was partially buried in the mud and the back wheels rested on a large boulder.

"How in the world did you miss not hitting the boulder head on?"

"I flew over it."

"The moon is silvery tonight. You almost don't need a flashlight. Why don't you go over there, just beyond that small clump of trees. You'll see the lake. It's a kind of resort. Find a bench to sit down and rest. You'll be fine. I'll look for your purse."

"I think I should help you look.

"You really should rest. You got quite a shake up."

"I can go back to the police car."

"Okay, here, take my hand. I'll lead you out."

Sara reached for Harp's hand. She felt his strong masculine grip tighten around her fingers.

"You're hurting me."

"You're too lovely for me to hurt."

Sara suddenly felt a tinge of fear. "Don't say that, please."

"I wanted you since my headlights first picked you up."

She wanted to run but she was petrified. "Please, let go of my hand." She tried to pull her hand from his, but he was too powerful for her feeble attempt. "I've got to get out of here."

He jerked her hard against his chest and forced his lips on hers, stifling an attempted scream.

"Do you know what a beautiful lady like you does to a man? You got no idea."

She pushed at him, but he squeezed her hand tighter and she heard the sound of her knuckles break.

"You broke my hand."

"I'll make it better. Just lie with me and you'll see how wonderful everything will be."

"Please. Please. Let me go or I'll scream."

"Who's gonna hear you? Another cop?"

"Aren't you afraid your partner will come here?"

"Who, Nick? He won't come. I never bother him when he picks up a junkie or a lady on call."

"Please, I beg you. Please. Let me go. I won't say a word. I promise."

"Just let me show you how I can love you, and everything will be all right. That's a promise I'll make."

"Please, I want to go home." Sara whimpered.

Harp, made his way up the embankment to find Nick dozing and clutching his empty coffee cup.

"Wake up and get rid of the coffee cup.

"Get your hands burned?"

"And kept my socks on."

"Was she good?"

"Couldn't get enough of me. Those rich dames really like it. You can call it in now. Tell 'em we found a female, thrown from her car. Dead."

THE SHARING OF THE FRUIT AND THE WINE

When I was a small boy, I'd spend Saturday afternoons with my Italian grandfather, a tall, strong, gentle man with a full, thick mustache. He'd take me to watch him play 'bocci ball' with his friends from the old country. When the games were over, we'd return home and sit at the kitchen table to share a piece of fruit and a glass of Grandpa's homemade wine. He'd sit in his chair beneath the ticking Roman-numerated wall clock.

I would push and maneuver my chair as close to his as I could and then wait anxiously for the ritual of the sharing to begin.

He'd ask me to pick out a piece of the fruit from the bowl on the table. I'd hand him a pear or an apple, and sometimes an orange. He'd take the fruit and hold it on its axis. After inspecting it for blemishes, he'd ask me where he should begin the peeling. I would point, then he'd reach around to his back pocket for his special peeling knife. He'd make the incision… and the magic would unfold. My heart would beat so fast as the fruit turned around and around and the peel, never breaking, curled about my grandfather's steady wrist.

Finally, the peel would fall to the white, enameled tabletop. He'd place a slice of the fruit in my glass of watered down wine. We would clink our glasses, and he would tell me another story about his growing up in the "old country" and of his long ocean voyage to reach America.

122

Luigi Filandino was proud to be an American citizen. He left his native land for the freedom of America. To cast his vote was his greatest treasure. He would say in his broken English, "God bless you, Juan, my American grandson." His accent would be on the J. I'd heard him say it so often, I just thought it was his way of talking to me. Besides, old people always said 'God Bless you.' I was too young to realize that in his broken English, he was expressing a grandfather's love. An affection I sense even today when I have any doubts or decisions confronting me.

"Grandpa, why do you always say that to me? About God and America?" I remember asking him one Saturday as we shared our fruit and wine.

"Because, you are born in America. Because you will grow up to be a strong man. A man who is free. Free to vote any way you choose. My Juan, you are too young to know what I say. But someday, you will know." I have never forgotten that moment.

My grandfather didn't earn a lot of money as a laborer. But he was an intelligent man. He worked hard during the spring and summer months, helping to build the Delaware Lackawanna Rail Road. During the ice and snow of winter when there was no laying of railroad tracks, he taught English to Italian immigrants, and Italian to second generation Americans, in his storefront school. But Saturday afternoons, he'd share with me. New arrivals from the old country would become members of his family until they were able to move into their own rented houses, many times taking with them, as a gift, an item from his household furnishings.

I believe God heard him whisper, "God bless you, Juan," because I grew up to enter the United States Navy during World War II. I became the man my grandfather wished. And "God bless you, Juan" sustained me, to return home unharmed.

One Saturday morning after I returned from the war, my grandfather's heart stopped. That afternoon, I sat in his chair under the Roman-numerated wall clock. I selected a bottle of his homemade wine from his cellar and placed it next to the bowl of fruit on the table. I poured two glasses and used his "special knife" to peel an orange. I clinked our glasses and whispered, "God Bless you, my American Grandpa."

Even though more than a half century has passed, I still hear the squish of his knife separating the peel from the pulp, the tick-tocking of the Roman-numerated wall clock. These sounds permeate my memory. No food or drink can be as delicious as our moments, sharing the fruit and the wine.

Spending Saturday afternoons with my grandfather filled a six-year-old boy with love and admiration that still generates a warm glow after these many years. A grandfather, who shares his time and shows his love for a small boy, shapes the man the boy becomes. There is no finality to his death. Whenever I cast my vote, and I always do, he accompanies me into the booth and I share the fruit and the wine once again.

***

ANGELS PLAY

He was afraid to open his eyes. Afraid he
might discover he was dead. The world was too
quiet, and he feared the sound of the silence. He
took a deep breath. The smell of burning flesh and
forest assured him he was alive. He opened his
eyes, slowly.

Trembling, he raised his head to survey his
immediate surroundings. The wind-tossed smoke
fumes limited his vision's range. What he was able
to see made him retch. Private Thomas W. Manes,
tenderfoot warrior, lay in a crater of decaying
bodies dressed in uniforms of bravery.

Weak from fatigue, he closed his eyes, lay
back and unwillingly surrendered himself into the
unconscious state of slumber. When he awoke, the
smoke and fire had died down and he could see,
more clearly, the devastating carnage his coming of
age manifested.

Lice feasted on his skin. Grime ringed his
neck, enticing swarms of flying insects to partake
communion of his skin. He was still too frightened
to raise a hand to swat his devourers. Any
movement—or the sound of a movement, he was
sure—would be followed by a volley of gunfire that
might end his life, so he let the vermin crawl over
him. He reasoned to himself that the little bastards
would only drown in the sweat oozing from his
pores anyway. With a silent prayer, he raised
himself a little higher to search the scorched scrub
for signs of something or someone alive. Nothing

stirred and no one had changed position. Was he the only mourner at the cremation of the world?

'No one is safe on the field of battle, Tommy, you know that. Did you hear the orders to hold your fire?' his inner voice spoke to him.

"I hope you're my guardian angel and not just my imagination. I need all the help I can get," he replied back to his inner voice. "I know someone's out there. I feel his snake eyes on me, like the fucking lice. If I could only see the bastard."

He prayed that if it came down to him or the sniper, that God would let him administer the last rites to the enemy.

He lay back down and took some more deep breaths, trying to see how long he could keep the air in his lungs. One of his high school coaches made him practice breathing whenever he got nervous before a game.

"Close your eyes and suck that oxygen, all the way down to your balls, and you won't fear nothin'." It always worked for him. Even here. Especially here, in the face of death.

When he opened his eyes again, he saw the remains of the charred tree. It had been there all this time, at the edge of the crater. "Hey, I didn't see you standing there. You must've been a proud sucker one time." His inner voice, jokingly, reminds him that he and the tree are like two peas in a pod. And probably have the same destiny.

"Hey, wait a minute. I can't think like that."

The urge to urinate was sudden and urgent.

"Jeez. I gotta go so bad. Oh, God! What am I gonna do?"

He opened his pants and turned on his side to relieve himself. "Dear Jesus, don't let him get me now." A broad grin broke on his face as he watched his urine turn the dry soil to mud. "That's all of me that I want to leave on this ground. "You hear that, Snake Eyes," he whispered a yell to his unseen adversary.

As he eased over on his back, he glanced skyward. He was stirred by the magnificence of the once lofty and proud tree. What had once been a harbinger of life and tranquillity made no promises of sanctuary to the young soldier.

"I gotta tree big as you in my back yard. Way back home. When I was a kid, I pissed up that sucker whenever I passed by it. So did my dog. His name was Jethro. But he's dead too, just like you. What I wouldn't give to be pissing up that tree right now."

Thomas W. Manes took another deep breath. "Coach, it ain't working. The quivering keeps comin' back. And this game ain't never gonna end."

He pushed himself up a little more, then unscrewed his canteen and raised it to his lips. He swallowed hard and rubbed the spout over his lips, enjoying the sensation of the snap and pull of his beard catching on the spout. He anticipated the hairs' springing back. He rubbed the canteen's spout across his lips again and again. The sound of the spout brushing against the hairs on his upper lip fascinated him. He'd invented his own little game within the grownup game of kill or be killed.

His mind drifted back to other games in other fields. Where white lines were drawn on green grass. Where he played by the rules and the only foe was the team from the rival school across town. And the only weapon was an oblong ball.

"Hey, Buddy," he reminded himself, "this is another game, on another field. The lines are drawn, and they ain't white. They can't be seen, but they're out there. Better be wary when I cross over them. In this game, on this field, the rule is, the quick get to stay alive."

In this game, Thomas W. Manes is being watched very carefully. He's been targeted and trapped in the crosshairs of a sniper's gun sight. His opponent has been waiting across the field, right about where Thomas imagined a goal post should be standing.

"Shit! I don't really know that I am alive. Maybe I am dead and waiting to be counted."

Terror has come to join him under the charred, barkless tree. He was scared that when the big game was over, he wouldn't be the one to pick up the toys and go home.

The tone of his inner voice startled him.

"Didn't you take a good long drink, dummy? You heard them hairs snap? Besides, you almost peed your pants. A dead man can't do those things."

His inner voice was tough and demanding. It always warned him whenever danger was near, telling him when to hold his breath. Whispering quietly, to be cautious. Screaming out, "Don't step there! Keep your head down. Hit that dirt and bear down. Bear down! Like you had a woman under you."

"What woman would want me now? I'm lice-picking dirty."

He tried hard to conjure up an illusion of himself with a woman. But he was too distressed. His fantasy blurred.

"All seems quiet out there. Too quiet to be peaceful."

He siphoned another mouthful from his half empty canteen.

"This water's warm as my piss."

He slid down and burrowed in a little deeper.

"Just sit tight for a while, Tommy."

The sniper inches forward.

"I can't see me gettin' out of this place."

He took another drink. He listened to the sounds the water made in his mouth as he swished it through his teeth, over his tongue and up under his upper lip, causing his nostrils to open wider. He bounced it from one cheek to the other, then sent it to the back of his mouth before he swallowed. The subtle noises his Adam's apple made as it jumped up and down to complete the swallow was a sound he hadn't heard since he was sucking at his mother's breast. Thomas closed his eyes and enjoyed the sensitivity and sounds of sucking.

The sniper squints his eye and watches the scaled down figure in his sights.

"I must be going crazy," Thomas told his inner voice. "Because of you, all I do is listen. I listen for the fall of a footstep, the silence of crickets. I even listen for the sound of unseen shadows hitting the ground. You got me afraid of the sounds of silence. Shut up and leave me alone."

He put the canteen to his lips again and slobbered.

The sniper adjusts his sights.

Thomas W. Manes felt the water dribble down his lips to his chin, forming a tributary to the sweat pools on his grubby neck.

"Ma!" he heard his voice call out. "If you could see me now. I've got a scraggily beard. A dirty maggot beard. Dirty clothes. Dirty body. Even my thoughts and my words are dirty. I live in a raunchy, vile, obscene world. An' it stinks. I stink. We all stink."

The breath of the sniper is heavy and steady.

"Momma, I play dirty games now. And sometimes when I go to sleep, I'm not clean. I even have dirty dreams. Momma, do you hear me? Dirty, scary nightmares of dying. Momma, do you know what I'd like to do?"

"No, my son. Tell Momma."

"I'd like to hose this rotten, skunk-smelling world down."

"All right, Thomas. I'll get some hot water and brown soap. We can start right here."

"I must be going nuts. Momma, don't answer me. Stay out of my dirty mind. You belong home. Where it's safe and clean."

The sniper takes aim.

"Listen, Ma. Hear that? I heard somebody's eyes blink." Something's going on out there. And I got no way to stop it."

"Thomas, be sure to wash good before going to sleep. Momma put clean sheets on the bed today. Remember, Thomas, angels play with clean little boys when they go to sleep.

Thomas felt the warmth of his mother's voice.

The sniper touches the slim, curved metal phallic of his rifle.

"Ma, I screwed up when I came over to this tree."

"Oh, Thomas, the way you talk. Let me tuck you in."

He feels the cool white sheets cover him.

"Momma, get away from here. Get away while you can."

The sniper squeezes his finger.

"Listen, Ma. Did you hear that?"

His mother begins to hum her lullaby.

"Momma, I think I got stung by something. Thomas reached up and touched his ear lobe. He felt the sticky, warm liquid oozing from his wound.

"Momma. I'm gonna die."

"Oh, Thomas, kiss Momma good night. Then close your eyes. Rest your head on Momma's breast, like you used to do when you were my little boy."

"Momma, tell me again. Will the angels come and play with me tonight? Even though I'm so dirty?"

"The Angels will surely come and play with you tonight, my son."

***

CRISTOBAL

She looked up at the slow moving Calder mobile dominating the art gallery and whispered, "Your beauty and power overwhelms me. I feel seduced standing here and I love you in return."

"I heard that," a voice came over her shoulder.

"You shouldn't eavesdrop on a lady and her lover."

"You shouldn't whisper so loud in an art gallery," a raspy masculine voice advised. "These walls have ears." His breath brushed her neck. "And they hang by your every word."

She turned toward the warm, sensual voice. "It's a majestic piece of work, don't you think?"

"They say it is. But to me it's just a giant pin-wheel."

"That's a terrible thing to say about great art."

"You think it's great art?"

"Yes. Of course I do."

"Well, I don't know anything about art. Good, bad or mediocre. But if you like it, it must be good."

"No. No. Art has to move you. You've got to feel something. It either excites you or it doesn't."

"Well, let's say I'll stand here while it moves, and look at you for my excitement."

"If you're not interested in art, what made you come here today?"

"The rain. And you?"

"I'm not working today. When I don't work I visit museums or movies, where they play the old, old films"

"Are you an artist?"

"In a way. I plan to be an actress. I go to auditions and answer cattle calls. But in the real world I'm just a waitress."

"You answer cattle calls? Here in New York?"

She laughed and took his arm, and led him to a bench. "A cattle call is an ad in the trade papers, advertising an open call for singers, dancers, ingenues. You know, performers."

"That's interesting."

"What about you."

"I guess you can say I'm an artist, in a way. I'm a designer in computer graphics."

"Computers. Wow, that's deep."

He let it go at that. If she thinks he's into something intellectual and complicated, he's made the right impression. "Whattya say, we get out of here. Go somewhere and have a coffee or something."

"Okay. There's a bar around the corner that's very cozy."

The barroom was dark and old fashioned. Soft orchestral tones filled the air, establishing an ambiance of quiet elegance. Another couple was discreetly secluded in a rear booth.

"Hi, Cristobal." The bartender greeted her as she approached the bar. "A white wine, I presume."

"Yes, thank you."

"The bartender knows your name?"

"Yes, he does."

"I'll accept that as a formal introduction. My name is—"

"Wait. Don't say it." She cut him short.

"Why? Don't you want to know my name?"

"No. You don't have a name, yet. When you do, I'll name you."

"You'll name me?"

"That's right. I'll give you your name."

"What is this, some kinda game?"

"No. I don't play games." She picked up her drink and walked across the room and slid into a booth. He enjoyed watching the way she swiveled as she walked away from him.

"Come sit next to me." She patted the empty seat next to her.

He put a ten spot on the bar and ordered a draft, then followed her scent.

"The barkeep said your name with a strange kind of accent," he said as he sat close to her. "I never heard 'Christabelle' said that way before."

"My name is not Christabelle. He said it right."

"With 'ball' on the end of it? Did you make it up for a stage name?"

"No. It's my name. My parents named me for the city where I was conceived and born, Cristobal, Panama."

"Panama? How come you don't have a Latino accent?"

"I grew up in England. But that's all you need to know." Her brusque reply conveyed her annoyance.

He wanted to touch her. Any part of her. Hands, fingers, thighs.

"So, what name are you gonna give me?" He ran his fingers through his hair, wishing she'd beg him to do the same to her.

"I don't know."

"You don't know?"

"That's what I said."

"That's a funny answer." "First, you say you're gonna give me a name, then you say you don't know."

"That's right. When and if I'm ready, you'll know."

"How long do I have to wait? I feel kinda incomplete walking around without a name, even for a minute."

"Maybe I won't want to give you a name at all."

"Excuse me, but I can't believe that. I think we hit it off, even if this is all kind of kooky." He sat so close to her he could almost feel the pores of her thighs. Her delicate mien, combined with her inherent kookiness, sent his center of gravity spinning out of control. He wanted to place his hands on her soft, smooth skin and experience a sensation of her vibrating up through his palms.

"It doesn't sound kooky to me. If I don't want to be with you anymore, all I have to do is get up and walk away. That way, you never entered my life and I won't have someone to forget or remember."

"And if you give me a name?"

"I'll never forget you."

"All right. I'll wait to be born again." He lifted his chilled beer mug to touch her stemmed white wine.

"The music is very much a part of the decor here. I come here some afternoons just to sit and listen to the melodies."

"More art appreciation?" He wanted to whisper words of passion to her as they lay together, not waste time on idle chatter in a bar.

"This is one of the few places in New York where you can hear that style of music."

"Music from the past. It's very nice. But it doesn't grab you. I like things that grab. If you know what I mean." *Please, Cristobal, come lie with me*, his whole being was begging.

She ignored his innuendo. "I'll tell you something about this bar. It has two lives."

"You gotta explain that one to me."

"All day long it is just an ordinary place. Where all types of people come. Office workers, tourists, even the cops, come here for lunch or a beer. But after eight o'clock at night, it takes on a whole new personality."

"Don't tell me it's haunted."

"No. It becomes a gay bar."

"Go on." He wasn't interested. *I just want to taste the aroma that is you.*

"It's true. That's why you're listening to the kind of music you are. You'll only find records of

Judy Garland and Barbra Streisand and some Montevani on that juke box."

"Millions of people like those records. That doesn't mean anything."

"I know. But this is New York. And New York ain't West Sqeedunk, New Jersey."

"Would you like another wine?"

"No. Please let me out."

He stood up for her to let her pass.

"Going to the little girls room?"

"No. I'm leaving now."

"You can't go." There was a little echo of panic in his voice.

"It's getting late. Bye."

Dear God, I can't loose her. "You can't leave me."

"Why not?"

"Because I'm in love and I haven't got a name."

***

Tragedians yearn to play for laughs, and Comedians aspire to play Hamlet. But if a singer is deprived of raising his voice in song, his whole life is an imitation, for he can never truly be himself.

—John Harrington Burns

CONVERSATION WITH A COMEDIAN

Just a few year ago before Las Vegas transplanted itself on the New Jersey shores, Skinny Damato's "500 Club" in Atlantic City was the most glamorous notorious watering hole outside of New York City and that desert gambler's mecca, Las Vegas.

I considered myself lucky to have been hired as the featured resident boy singer and emcee for the shows in the main dining room where the East Coast Mafia and the Hollywood stars gathered. That's where I met Joe E. Lewis, the celebrated television and nightclub comedian. Joe E. would tell you himself that he was a drinker first and then a comedian. And he drank hard. He never walked on stage unless there was a table with a bottle of booze and a glass set right up there, sharing the spotlight with him. When the bottle was empty, he'd interrupt his monologue and walk into the audience and steal a patron's drink—sometimes right out of their hands—and chug-a-lug it down before the poor perplexed customer knew what was happening. He'd then get back on stage and continue with his jokes, to the applause and approval of an appreciative house.

One night after the show, he invited me to join him for a drink. Being young, ambitious and impressionable and slightly star struck, I agreed wholeheartedly. I was all set to go over to one of the after-hour bars where all the musicians and performers playing in town congregated, including the chorus girls. I figured we'd have few drinks and pick up a couple of broads. It would be easy with a celebrity like Joe E. Lewis. But instead, he lead me out through the back stage door of the club and into the dim, dank alleyway where a couple of galley employees were arranging garbage cans and picking up the litter-strewn pavement. Joe E. looked around, then walked over to a dark corner and sat down. His back rested against one of the garbage pails and his legs stretched out before him. He reached under his jacket and pulled out a plain brown bag.

"Come on, kid. Sit down over here next to me."

The stench of garbage permeated the early morning air and stung my nostrils. My companion in this excursion into the lower depths sat opposite me, lovingly caressing a bottle of his favorite libation.

"Joe, is this your idea of a fun night?"

"Come on, sit down." His voice had a heavy rasping guttural quality.

"Joe, this ain't my idea of how to spend the night."

"I told you I got something I want to tell you, and this is the place. I can't mingle in crowds. It's too uncomfortable to be around too many people."

"Joe, I hope you ain't got any funny ways I never suspected."

"Nah, kid, don't worry. I ain't one of those guys if that's what you're thinking. I just want to tell you something."

"What the hell," I thought. "I'll humor the guy for a few moments before I'd chalk it up to a bad experience and take off." I sat down amid the garbage.

One of the cleanup crew came and began sweeping. "Hey, it's all wet there. We just hosed that place down. Now we gonna sweep it out to the street. We gonna hose some more. Sit there and you're gonna get washed away too. It's up to you."

Joe E. kept on drinking from the paper bag and just waved him off. Like a fool, I sat in puddles of water with the world-famous comedian who found his pleasure from a plain brown paper bag.

"I like you, kid."

He called me kid, I think, because he really didn't care who I was. I was just someone to talk to.

"You got a great talent and I'm jealous." He lifted the bottle up to his lips and took a swig, then ran his sleeve across his lips to sponge his drool.

"You jealous of me? You? You're Joe E. Lewis. You do the Ed Sullivan Show. Millions of people laugh at your jokes."

"No. It's true. I envy you."

"You're putting me on."

"Anybody can get up and tell a few dirty jokes."

I began to wonder what the hell he was up to, telling me he envied me. Water was beginning to soak through my tuxedo to my skin.

"I got a million dirty jokes. Everybody laughs. So what?"

I remember how his head dropped and he grew silent for a moment.

"But when you sing, people stop and listen. They get dreamy eyed. And maybe some of them fall in love. Right there on the dance floor." I didn't know what to say, so I raised the bag to my lips.

He reached over, grabbed my arm and pulled the bottle down from my lips. His eyes seemed to search mine and I could see the expression of a troubled man. It was as though I was seeing his soul. It frightened me.

"What you got is something wonderful."

"Joe, you're making me uncomfortable."

"There's a wariness to your voice that just falls off your lips and into the lady's ear every time you inhale and sing out with that warm sound you got. I used to have that."

Through the raspy, broken-glass sound of his voice, I heard the sadness in his heart.

"Now all I got are wisecracks and snide remarks. I say anything to get them to laugh. I hate when they look at me. You'll never know that feeling."

A couple of more workers came out and began to sweep. The whisking of the brooms against the pavement was a low-keyed murmur, threatening us to get up and leave or be swept out with the wet gutter debris.

I got up and tried to help Joe E. rise and stand on his feet, but he resisted my efforts and became belligerent.

"Come on, Joe," I begged. "It's almost sunrise and these guys want to get done and go home. Let me call you a cab."

One of the sweepers grabbed Joe E. under his left arm and helped me hoist him up against the building.

"My name is Tony. I'm a nobody bus boy; this guy's got his name in lights out front of this building. And every night, him and I are here with the garbage. If I made his money, no way I'd be here. Can't figure out some guys." The sweeper continued. "He talks to himself and waves the vodka around and then he tries to sing. You ever hear him sing? Sounds like an elephant with hiccups. Terrible"

"He's okay. Just give me a hand."

"You hang out with him and you're looking at yourself a ways down the road."

I was listening to advice from a bus boy. I really was on a down elevator at top speed.

"If I were you, I'd dump this guy and get myself a cab and head on home." He kept right on talking while he helped me to get Joe E. to stand up. "Don't worry about him. Bums like him always manage to get home one way or another."

We got Joe E. propped up against the wall of the building. "Well, he's up. Don't know for how long. I'm gonna go now. Call it quits. Hope I don't see you out here tomorrow morning."

He turned and walked out of the darkness of the alley into the early morning light of the street beyond.

"Don't listen to him," Joe started again, "'cause I do got something to tell you. Sit down and listen. Then I'll let you call a cab and I'll go home. And I'll never bother you again."

144

"Joe, don't you think you can tell me tomorrow when you're sober?"

"I'm never soberer than I am right now. You know I'm always drunk. Now I got to tell you. I got to. Every time I see someone like you, it hurts me."

I tried to interrupt him but he wouldn't let me cut him off.

"I used to have a beautiful voice. A really good voice. When I sang, I sang right from here." He pounded his chest. "Heart. I had plenty of heart. And I put it all into my songs. But those dirty sons of bitches. What they did to me."

He started to cry and slowly slid down the wall and crumbled to the ground. I put my hands on his shoulders and quietly asked him to stop crying. I was embarrassed and self-conscious. I really didn't know how to help him. He looked at me, then he turned away and let the sobs come from every atom of his being.

After a while, the sobs stopped and Joe began in a soft whisper. "They cut my throat."

He untied his bow tie and ripped open his shirt and raised his chin. "See? That's what they did to me." He drew his finger from his right ear lobe down his neck and around his Adam's apple and up to his left ear lobe. The long, gnarled scar seemed like a seam sewn by a blind man. Joe E. caught me as I averted my eyes.

"See? Not even you can look at it. Can you imagine how it repulses a woman. That's why I always go home alone." He sobbed.

"Who cut your throat, Joe? Who did it?" I asked him. The pit of my stomach tightened and I began to tremble. It might have been the reaction from the booze, I don't know, but I think it was all the pain and sadness I discovered in the man that touched a chord of sympathy within me.

"The mob did, that's who," he answered. "Some lousy gangsters. And for what? For what?"

I looked again at the long, ugly scar tissue that covered the damage of a cut that not only severed his vocal cords but left lesions on his soul.

"For what?" He kept repeating. "I'll tell you what for. All because I was singing in one club and bringing in the crowds. Some rival mobster decides to kidnap me and cut my throat, just to show me he's the boss: if I won't sing in his club, I won't sing in anybody's club. I won't sing anymore, period. I can't sing anymore, kid. I can't sing anymore." He began to sob again, and this time there was nothing I could do or say to console him. Just being there was all he wanted of someone. I could only experience this particular moment in time with him. The horror that was alive in his mind was his alone.

"Joe, please calm down. You made it anyway. You're on top. So fuck them."

"It's an easy thing to say, 'Fuck them.' I thought you would understand. When I hear a song inside my head, I hear it with my real voice. I think of how I would phrase it, how I would put it over and sell it. I hear the whole orchestra arrangement and me singing with the voice I was born with. Not this mutated, strangling noise that comes out when I sing a little on stage just to get a laugh. When I sing,

I want to sound like you, not like an ass braying and thinking he sounds like a canary."

I decided to keep silent and let him get it out of his system.

"Like an animal being slaughtered, that's what it was like. Like an animal in a slaughterhouse. Only they didn't leave me to die. They wanted me to live. They punished me because I had a beautiful voice. Why didn't I die? Why didn't they put a bullet through my brain? They wouldn't kill me, but they killed the only thing that was important to me. I hope they rot in hell. That's where they are, you know. They're dead. One of them got the electric chair. I hope he burned and is still burning in hell."

As I watched him crumble, the night was slowly fading into a pearl gray blanket of morning mist.

"Let me get a cab and we'll go down to the beach and watch the sun come up and get some clean air in our lungs. And maybe flush ourselves out. What do you say? We get out of this depressing unclean atmosphere.

"Okay. But no cab. I'll show you I can carry on drunk or sober. I'm gonna walk." So we walked down Missouri Avenue, staggering and leaning on each other. I don't remember clearly enough to say that we didn't fall down a couple of times, but I do remember my pants were still wet and clinging to my skin, making the walk physically uncomfortable.

When we reached the beach, Joe and I sat on a boardwalk bench and watched the waves pounce and play tag with the wading birds. The sun was rising in an orange sky. A few bicycle riders passed behind us, and the pancake and coffee merchants were setting up for the early morning breakfast vacationers.

"I used to be a singer, you know, kid," Joe E. said. He was repeating himself. He probably forgot what he just went through back there in the alley.

"Yes, I heard."

"Do you know why I don't sing anymore? And don't say, 'Because you got a lousy voice.'" He was very serious.

"Joe, I'm going over to one of the stands and get us a cup of coffee. Black. Okay?"

"Okay, but hurry back. I don't like to be alone too long around all this water. It ain't good for my image."

I went over and purchased the coffee, and when I turned to walk back to Joe E., I walked very slowly because I didn't want the hot coffee spilling and burning my hands, and second, to reflect upon the impact the last few hours had had on me. And I wondered about Joe E. Lewis. All he'll want is his liquor. And all he'll ever have is conversations with guys like me. I'm sure I wasn't the first alley bum he found to commiserate with, and I am positive I wouldn't be the last. It just happened that I was one who worked nearest to him on stage, so I guess he grabbed me to share his story.

But now here at the ocean's edge, he was sitting with his back to me on a bench, hunched over and bent. He looked like a man defeated and spent. Suddenly, he wasn't the magnificent star I stood on stage with every night and bantered a few jokes with and sang a line or two of his routine. He was just a lonely man lost in a sea of laughing people who wanted him only as a buoy for their survival while he was trying in desperation to grab onto the life ring that he expected them to throw out to him. But it wasn't working that way. He was drowning and they were looking past him and never heard his cries.

I sobered up. Maybe it was the sea air, but I was determined that I was not going down with him. I knew how to swim and that was my conveyance to survival.

I handed Joe the coffee and sat down beside him.

"Did I tell you I'm writing a book about my life, and already, some Hollywood people have approached me about a movie deal? It's all pretty hush-hush right now."

"No, Joe, you didn't."

"Maybe you can play me in the movie. But you know those Hollywood people, they will want a big name like Damone or Sinatra. If I had a say in it, I'd want you to do it, because you're fresh and naïve. Like I was before they cut the songs out of my life."

"Joe, let me go get you a taxi."

"No," he said. "I think I'm gonna stay awhile longer and experience daylight. You know, I don't get to see too much of life in the daytime. Look, kid, it's true: people really do come out when it ain't dark. Don't tell anybody I said this, but sometimes a little water makes a good chaser." He extended his hand to include the Atlantic Ocean.

I left him there and went home to get some sleep.

That night on stage, he came on the way clowns always came on, ready for the show with his familiar trademark "Voom Voom. Voom Voom." And a million dirty jokes up his sleeve.

*

Epilogue: A few years later, the movie, 'The Joker Is Wild,' starring Frank Sinatra as Joe E. Lewis, was made.

***

Bold, ambitious young men and women break from their roots to seek fortune and fame in cold, unfriendly big cities. Those who are less daring and not as eager, stay and dig their roots deeper to enrich the folklore, good or bad, of our beginnings. They become the oral fables we pass on to the next generation. Such is the story of...

VERNA

On my way to Germany to cover the dismantling of the Berlin Wall, I had a couple of hours lay over at Newark Airport. As is my habit, I wandered over to the newsstand to see if I might recognize a by-line of a colleague. I skimmed the top half of the folded Newark Star Ledger. Nobody I knew made the headlines. I turned the paper over to check out the bottom half. I was about to put it down when I saw Verna's name. Verna, a childhood hero of mine, was killed in a barroom brawl and misidentified as a male. Her sex wasn't noticed until her body was examined at the morgue. She died as she lived: rough, tough and aggressive, dressed in men's clothing. Her death, like her life, was controversial.

I read her story with deep sadness. Verna and I came from the same neighborhood. We go back a long way, even though she's a generation older.

It was right about this time last year that I last saw Verna. I hadn't been back home in a hell of a long time. After the war, I was restless. The sand in my shoes kept me walking. Somehow, as far as I wander, a path leads back to old familiar haunts.

I remember it was a Saturday night. The thunder of an approaching rain greeted me as I stepped out of the White Castle. I paused a moment in the light of the street lamp to reflect and let my memory control the moment. In the chilly, damp air, my imagination watched a spark spewing and a metal, screeching trolley car come rattling down Central Avenue once more. I listened hard to hear the echo of its clanging bells. But the sound was too distant. The trolley tracks had been dug up for scrap iron, turned into ammunition and sent off to war, along with all the able-bodied young men of the town.

The newsstand, to my surprise, was still there. I walked over and picked up a New York Sunday Times and the local newspaper, along with a magazine. I lay down a fiver and waited for my change.

"Put your hand in your pocket, mister. We don't give no change here."

"My God!" I said, half aloud, "It's Verna the Bear." I recognized a familiar face from out of the past. It was really good to be home again.

"Hey, Verna! I should get at least a quarter plus back"

"You keep hangin' around here, wise ass, and I'll come out and bust you right in your fuckin' face."

Same old Verna: no punches pulled and a language I could understand. She got her name, The Bear, one summer night when the carnival came to town. A ten-dollar prize went to anyone who would stay five minutes in the ring, wrestling a bear. To the chagrin of her family, Verna stepped out of a cheering crowd to meet the challenge...and won the prize.

"Verna, you don't remember me? I remember you from the old days."

"It's dark and my eyes ain't so good. Should I know you?"

"Remember Packy?"

"Packy? Never forget him. Had the voice of an angel. Sang on the radio. So, who the hell are you?"

"I'm his son."

"Snot-nosed kid with the freckles? Played baseball?"

"Yeah."

"Still play baseball?"

"Whenever I get the chance. How about you?"

"Nothin' but a bunch of fairies around here. They don't know a bat from their dicks."

If Verna had been a man, and there are some who had their doubts, she would be retired today from the majors. She hurled a ball with such speed and power it burned the catcher's mitt and left a batter twisted and turned, wondering what the hell flew by. When she got her turn at bat, she'd send that ball high over the stadium bleachers and right on out to the street. Broke a hell of a lot of windshields.

"Let's get a closer look at you." She came out from behind her makeshift counter. "Kid, I'm gettin' up in years. My eyes ain't what they used to be."

She put her face up close to mine. Her face was lined and dirty and her breath had a tinge of booze. She was dressed the way she always dressed: men's shoes and pants, a soiled Navy Pea coat, and a Navy woolen watch cap pulled down over her ears. And she smelled.

"I just wanna see who you look like, your father or your mother. I remember her too. Beautiful woman." She squinted. "You're all right. Don't have their special good looks, though."

Her voice sounded as though it had to travel up from down deep in her midsection and filter through several layers of stones and gravel before the words formed and reached their destination.

"Kid, even if you are who you say you are, I don't make change. Can't you see the sign right there." She pointed to a metallic, engraved sign holding down a stack of papers. "Maybe you don't read too good. But it says 'EXACT FARE NO CHANGE' in big fuckin' letters." She turned from me, and limped to her place behind the counter.

It saddened me to see a giant from my youth shrinking to human size. I pulled my collar up close to my face to shield me from an occasional drop of rain.

"Get that from one of the trolley cars you used to work on?"

"What the hell do you know about trolley cars?"

I sensed hostility waiting to escape from an unpredictable character, so I decided to steer the conversation in another direction before I walked away and returned Verna the Bear to her place in my memory.

"How's Pete doing?" I sent out a friendlier feeler and moved away from her workspace.

Verna and Pete were always together. If they were lovers, I don't know. Pete, a professional pallbearer, was amiable and unpretentious. Never said a word unless he was answering a direct question. And when he spoke, his voice was soft and almost inaudible. He had the loyalty and devotion of a pampered pet. He followed Verna everywhere.

Suddenly, I remembered one long lost summer day; my old man's Studebaker blew a tire. We waited for a state trooper or some kind of roadside service to come to our aid. But none came, until Verna and Pete came riding by in her old jalopy.

"What the hell's wrong, Packy?" she growled. Cigarette smoke filtered through her nose.

"Got a blown tire, Verna. And I got no jack. Been waiting for the troopers to come by so we can get some help."

"Forget the friggin' cops," Verna said in her coarse and hardened way. "I got a jack." She got down on her knees and unbolted the wheel. "Now, I'm gonna lift the car. When I tell you, take the flat tire off and put on the good one."

"Verna, you can't lift this car."

"Who sez I can't? Just watch me."

"Maybe Pete could help you lift," my concerned, fretful father suggested.

"Pete? Are you kiddin'? Pete has trouble liftin' Little Pete."

"Verna!" My father blushed.

I watched, amazed and in awe, as Verna lifted the back end of the Studebaker off the ground.

She held it steady while my poor old man struggled to place the good tire on the wheel. Never once did Verna take the dangling, smoking cigarette from her lips. And never once did Pete utter a word or move a muscle as he sat and watched from the passenger seat of Verna's car.

A slight drizzle brought me back to reality as I heard Verna say, with a hint of affection, "The poor old son of a bitch up and died on me." Her eulogy was resentful and yet touchingly remorseful.

"I'm sorry."

"So I went and got me a couple of new boarders to stay out at the house. A couple of live ones are better than one in the grave."

Sporadic raindrops nudged me to move out from her workspace. Cars began pulling up to the curb, and a few pedestrians rushed up to the stand for their papers. Those who put down the exact amount she castigated for being too cheap to leave a tip. Those who expected change she chased away with a few choice words that stung their eardrums harder than any ball she ever pitched. Townsfolk who knew her had their correct change ready and ignored the source of the roar. It was only those who happened to have the misfortune of stopping by her newsstand by chance who were truly frightened by her ferocious demeanor and crude language. She was as predictable as mercury. Tough as leather one moment and as soft and as gentle as a child's smile the next. To me, she was the hometown's tarnished treasure.

The drizzle matured into a somber downfall. I lingered like a voyeur, unabashedly deriving

157

pleasure from Verna's badgering and insulting her customers. Maybe it was because I harbored a childhood admiration for my friend of yesteryear.

Reluctantly, I left Verna hawking her papers and took a nostalgic drive along familiar streets. Reliving some moments of my youth. Hoping I would see an old friend. But my headlights only picked up melancholy raindrops and shadows of yesterday.

Sleep didn't come gently to me that night. Verna touch me in the darkness. A young unlined face smiled at me with eyes that sparked with capricious mischief. I asked her where her smiles had gone now. But she didn't answer.

The next morning, I went down to the old neighborhood. I treaded the tracks of the Lackawanna Railroad that wended alongside Madison Avenue and Bell Street. I walked through the cement factory I used to use as a short cut on my way to school. Although the plant is abandoned and in disrepair today, the lingering odor of powdered cement hung so heavy I could taste it. I emerged from an exit directly opposite Verna's house.

In the high-noon sunlight, the house shone like a silent, powerful caveat. The upper portion of the building was dotted with huge white stars on a field of blue. The second and first stories were painted in stripes of red and white. American flags flew from every porch stanchion and fence post around the property. It was unmistakably Verna's house, a house that welcomed any homeless person, bum or railroad hobo, to enter and rest, but like a beacon, sent a warning to those who came bearing malice. Several vigilante dogs patrolled the chain-link fenced enclosure.

Curiosity is my livelihood. As a writer, I was instinctively impelled to climb those porch stairs and knock on that door. I had to get inside the house and walk through the rooms and corridors of Verna's life. As I neared the house, the barking, menacing dogs threatened my every step. Even though they were enclosed, their bark scared the hell out of me. The stench of dog feces that littered the yard eradicated the lingering smell of cement from my nostrils.

The porch door opened. "Hey, you at the gate. If you're selling something, we don't want it."

Because of the bright sun, I couldn't make out who it was. "I'm a friend of Verna's," I yelled over the din of the dogs.

"Verna ain't got no friends. G'way."

"Verna? That you? It's me, Packy's boy. I saw you last night. Remember?"

"So? What the fuck y'want now?"

"Just thought I'd say hello."

"You said it. G'bye."

"Wait. Don't close the door. I want to ask you something. But the dogs are making too much noise."

Verna came down and shooed the dogs. "That's why I got 'em. Keeps pricks like you away. The yard's loaded with shit, so watch where you step. Don't want you bringing it in my house."

She unlatched the gate and, to my surprise, led me up the walk and onto the porch . The porch was jammed, packed with tied-up bundles of newspapers, garbage and dog feces. She opened the door and ushered me into a hall that led to a back kitchen. On the right, was a staircase leading up to the second-floor bedrooms. The parlor was off to the left. A dining room was just beyond an archway.

"Let's go in the parlor." She pointed the direction. There were a couple of sofas and three cots in the room. I expected clutter, but the house was neat.

"Them cots are for the homeless men. The women and kids, I send upstairs on the beds. Poor suckers ain't got nothin'." She actually sounded like an old softy for a second. Then she caught herself and reverted to her crusty personality. "I got some tight-assed neighbors who don't like what I do. They want me out of their sight. So I upgraded my property by painting my house the colors of our flag. It only made them madder. Shoulda made them proud. Now, what the fuck you wanna ask me?"

I really had nothing to ask or say, even though all kinds of questions, anecdotes and statements were running through my mind. She had me. So I blurted out the first thing that came to my mind. "What the hell makes you so angry and hostile?"

"You do."

"Me?"

"And everybody like you. Your kind think you own the whole fuckin' world. Well, you don't. And I'm gonna remind you that there's me, Verna, to put you down a notch when you get high and mighty."

"That's not true. You don't hear me or anyone else dot their sentences with foul language, like you do, just to intimidate people."

"The fuck you don't. You guys make me laugh. You intimidate just by having balls. You're foul when you bark orders. You push and shove, expecting us to run, hop and jump, just because you can growl deeper. Well, you can't do that to me. I can play your fuckin' game without your ammunition. And I can hit the mark. Where it hurts."

"Where's that fun-loving Verna who pounded so hard on our door early one Sunday morning. I thought my old man would shit a brick, or have a heart attack. He jumped out of bed so fast to run and open the door. Never asked who was there. He just yanked that damn door so fast and hard. And all of a sudden your huge Greyhound tumbled down on him, his slobbering tongue licking the old man's face and bald head. It still makes me laugh whenever I think of it."

Verna cracked a slight smile. "I stood that dog up against the door so that when it opened, his paws would land on Packy's shoulders. I was down in the stairwell laughing my ass off. Never heard Packy swear like that before."

"Neither did I. 'There's only one person who would do such a thing,' he said. 'That effen Verna.'"

"Just like Packy. He never used the real word. He's one guy I really liked. That's the only reason I let you in the door. Otherwise, I'da sent you on your fuckin' way."

"I'm curious as to why you terrorize people and bully them into buying your papers, then you scare the shit out of them when they want their change. Even when I was younger, I remember you selling papers in the trolley cars. When you got on, half the car got off before their stops just to get away from your threatening them. Even little kids went running and screaming when they saw you walking toward them. What happened to make you mean and angry?"

"I ain't mean. A little angry maybe, but I ain't mean. Let me show you something, buster." She led me over to the mantle on the other side of the room. "See this picture here?" She took down a framed, faded photo from the mantle and handed it to me. "That's Mayor Fiorella La Guardia of New York City shaking my hand. That bicycle between us is the bike that I rode all the way from San Francisco to New York. The Mayor hisself greeted me. Never got in the papers the way it was supposed to, because of a fuckin' printer's strike. I did things in my day women didn't do. I worked the trolleys, climbed poles, worked choppin' down trees. Shit, I even sparred rounds with the light-weight contender, Spider Moran. I didn't stay home and wear no fuckin' apron. I did things."

"I know you did. I think what you did was great. I only mean—"

"You don't know what you mean, because you don't know your ass from a hole in the ground," she cut me off. "You're just a nosy son of a bitch, looking for a story. So don't say 'I only mean.' If I was Babe Didrikson, I'da been

somebody, and you'da had a good story. So don't
shoot your mouth off askin' what happened to me."

"You gotta admit people think you act
crazy."

She jerked her head and let out a gasp when
she heard the word. I wished I could have grabbed it
in midair and stuffed it back in my mouth. But it
was too late. Verna's face drained of all color, her
lips paled and trembled.

"I ain't crazy," she whispered. Her glazed
eyes darted from one side to the other as if looking
for an exit to escape a flaming building. But this
was her house. She was safe. I was the one who
should've been looking for an escape route.

"Don't call me crazy," she spewed.
"Waddya know about crazy? You shit head."

"I didn't say you were crazy. I said—"

"I heard what you said. I been to the crazy
house. Y'know that? And nobody put me there. I
went there myself. I ain't there now."

"Verna, forget it. I'm gonna go now." I wore
the colors of cowardice. I looked for my escape
route along the baseboard of the floor.

"You ever been to the crazy house? Huh?"
She clasped her hands and stretched her arms out in
front of herself. "There ain't nothing to do there but
go crazy."

I saw the tears poise on her lashes waiting to
fall. I was ashamed that I used the ruse of friendship
to reduce this fragile, craggy volcano of uncertain
emotions to bare herself before my eyes.

"That's where my mother died."

Her simple reply cut me. "I didn't know"; I offered a hollow condolence. Verna's surfaced vulnerability made me aware of an emerging malicious quality in my nature more gross than her outward belligerent aggression. I grew anxious and, quite honestly, a little frightened. She was panting and hyperventilating. I didn't know what to expect next.

"I went there too." She reeled slightly. "I lived there, like she did."

Anticipating her fall, I moved closer to her.

"I go there whenever I feel myself falling apart."

I took her arm and led her over to the sofa.

"I sign myself in and I sign myself out."

I steadied her into the upholstered chair. She sat with her knees apart, like an old man after a hard day in the fields. Visibly distressed, she rubbed her hands on her thighs. She stopped and caught her breath. Her mood became quite dark and morose.

She closed her eyes and said quietly, "You know they got a farm there?" She never stopped rubbing her thighs. "If you ain't locked in a padded room or sitting with your hands wrapped around your waist." Her words came jerky and haltingly. "You ever been bound up in a straight jacket?"

I just stared at her. I couldn't answer. Sometimes I hated my profession, because it robbed me of being some person I could have been: an ordinary, everyday man instead of a man probing and searching, never cognizant of others; just get the story. That's what I was doing to poor Verna and I let the whole situation get out of hand. I wasn't even a good reporter. Damn! How did I let it go this far?

"You can't move your hands, can't scratch you ass… can't wipe the tears from your eyes. When you can answer me, then maybe you can have the right to ask me any questions. But you ain't been there, you prick.

I tried to hide in the silence that descended.

She clenched her fists tightly and dug her knuckles into her thighs and pushed against herself, throwing her head back. She gasped and grabbed at her knees and brought them up to her chest and buried her head between her knees.

She slowly raised her head and flashed me a sardonic smile. "But me…," she continued methodically, as she resurrected a memory she had buried deep in the chasms of her mind, hoping she would never have to resurrect it, ever again. Slowly, she began. "They put me in with the horses. Ever see what happens to them stallions at night?"

She was too disconcerted for me to answer. I humbly shook my head.

"Believe me, nature ain't pretty in a stall. They gave me a pail. My job was to listen for the horses to take a piss. Then I hadda run real quick and find the pissing horse and fill up the pail. Sometimes, two or three would let go at once. I'd run around, dropping pails and getting pissed on. The noise and the stench.…" She paused and stared off, focusing her eyes on something only she could see. "I hate the fuckin' four-legged things."

"Verna, please… you don't have to go on."

"They sell the pee, y'know." She continued to speak as if she were alone and remembering a nightmare, reciting it to purge it from her mind. "They use the piss for medicine. That's what they told me."

The tears made their way down her wrinkled cheeks. I wanted to kneel before her and wipe away all the tears of her life, but I just stood there and listened as she slowly and painfully flayed and gutted her life. A life that never asked for pardons. A life that ached to be understood before it died. A life that was never embraced by the warmth of love.

"Once, a couple of silly-assed women asked me if I was really a homorfidite. It was on Main Street, in front of the Brill Sisters Photo Studio. I grabbed them two bitches by their arms and pushed them into the studio. Scared the bejesus outta them. And right there, in front of the photographer, I stripped down. 'Take a good look,' I told them. 'You don't see no lavaliere hanging on me. I'm more woman than any one of you will ever be.'"

"You didn't."

"I sure fuckin' did. They about fainted." A tiny sparkle gleamed for a second and she grinned before she her face broke into a smile.

I laughed and she joined me. Her laugh was hearty and full-throated, deeper than mine. But like quicksilver, she turned ugly. "Now, get the fuck outta my house, you two-faced bastard. I know your kind. A fuckin' mind doctor, looking for a guinea pig. Well, I ain't falling for your shit."

I got up and started to leave. Before I reached the door she called out, "And don't ever bring your sorry ass back here again. You ain't nothing like Packy."

As my plane climbed higher and left New Jersey far beneath, I settled in my seat and leaned back to enjoy my memories of Verna. I visualized her posing nude for the ladies at the Brill Sisters Photography Studio. I sneaked a glance out the window, because you never know with Verna. She's brazen enough to show up just to give me the finger from the other side.

I laughed and I heard her join me. Her laugh was hearty and full-throated, much deeper than mine.

***

THE CHOSEN SEX

He watched through half-closed eyes as she rose from their bed. He inhaled every delicious movement as she strode across the room to adjust the blinds. To see the sunlight come in and touch her shoulders and highlight her hair ignited an implosion within him a million times more fervent than those countless sun-sent atoms. In spite of their timeless devotion and intimate familiarity, she still retains her feminine aura of mystery he knows he will never penetrate or fathom.

She bent over the supposedly sleeping man and brushed her lips to his ear to seductively whisper, "I know you're awake."

The warmth of her breath tenderly caressed him. He mumbled something incoherently, and then he fully opened his eyes, sheepishly grinned and longingly gazed at her.

"With your bending over me and the way the sunlight touches your hair, reminds me of that painting you've always wanted. What's it called again?

"It's called 'Daybreak,' by Maxfield Parrish." She sat on the side of the bed. "What a lovely thought. That's what this morning is, our Maxfield Parrish daybreak. It kind of sets a warm, wonderful mood for the whole day. I'll make breakfast if you're ready to rise up."

He laughed and chided her over the double entendre. "Come back to bed," he pleaded, hoping she would but knowing she would ignore his request. "It's lonely in here."

She smiled and started to leave. He rolled over and wrapped his arms around her. She didn't resist. She fingered his hair, remembering that it used to be a solid color just a short time ago. Now it was dusted with gray and thinning. She held his face in her hands and kissed him on his chin. "You need a shave, Mister Gray Beard."

"You mean, if I shave and put on the after shave you like so much, I'll get lucky?"

"No, you won't get lucky."

"Well, I guess you just don't love this old gray beard as much as you say you do."

"Oh, I don't love you anymore? Is that why I'm so willing to prepare and serve you breakfast?" She lifted the sheet and got back into the bed. "You men."

"What's that supposed to mean, 'You men.'"

"You're funny. You're always ready to be adolescently virile and you get so fiercely offended if your masculinity is treated lightly."

"That's just a feminine notion."

"No, my dear. It is a fact."

"You can't prove it by me."

"Especially by you."

He lay back on the pillow and stared up at the ceiling. Neither one spoke for a minute or two.

"You've very quiet for a hungry man."

"Just thinking about us." He turned and raised himself on his elbow. "You and me. A lot of breakfasts have come and gone, haven't they?"

She caressed his face and rubbed her nose against his. "Yes, but there are so many more to look forward to."

"Do you ever let your mind take you back to our first breakfast together?"

"If you're going to mention the morning I dropped the poached eggs out of the pan onto your lap, yes. I see that scene in my mind and I shrug with horror. Then I burst out laughing."

"Good grief, did I yell. You almost poached more than those eggs. I thought our love life was over right then and there. No, I didn't mean then." His fingers traveled up along the lapel of her dressing gown. He rubbed the flimsy material between his thumb and forefinger. The feel of the feminine fabric pleasured him. "We were married when you did that to me. I meant before we were married. When we lived in that place, you know, over the barber shop around the corner from the main campus."

"Not a day of my life goes by that I don't think of us there in that flat with the red and white revolving barber's pole right outside our entrance. That's a part of our lives that no one else shares. No one. I like to think of it as the beginning of you and me. From that first day forward until this minute."

His fingers traced the outline of her ear and traveled down along her lovely neck to rest in the cleavage of her bosom. "And into the tomorrow's to come."

"You are my life." She touched his finger and took his hand and held it to her breast.

"Thank you for saying that. I love you, you know, and I do take advantage of you. I've kind of grown accustomed to you catering to me. Many times I want to stop and say thanks, but I don't. Do you know why I don't?"

She shook her head.

"Because I'd go around all day long thanking you. Neither one of us would have time for anything else. Not even moments like this."

"Well, I wouldn't go so far as to say that. An occasional 'thank you' would be nice. But your saying you might get lucky is thanks enough for me. It tells me I'm still desirable to you after all these years. She took his hand from her bosom and playfully bit the tips of his fingers.

A hush came over the sun-bright room.

He sat up and began to speak, then hesitated, unsure of how to say the sentence he saw clearly in his mind. When he finally spoke, his words came slowly. "I know I am not going to say this right, but I have often wondered...." He paused mid-sentence and took a deep breath. He felt the beads of perspiration break through the delicate parts of his anatomy. He couldn't believe that, at his age, he would become too embarrassed to ask his lover an intimate question. "Forget it."

His sudden blush of red intrigued her. "Go on. Don't stop now. I'm anxious to find out what would make you blush and stammer so."

"Oh, it's nothing. The whole question sounds terrible. I take it back."

"Don't you dare take it back. It seems that this is not an impulsive question. You probably have been wanting to ask it for some time."

"Well, I was wondering if you ever had any trepidation about sleeping with me the very first time," he blurted out in one fast expulsion of breath, relieved, in a sense, that it was out and spoken.

She looked away. After a pensive moment, she turned and faced him. "Why would I have those feelings? I planned that you would be my lover way before you even knew who I was. The only thing that I was afraid of was that you'd discover how brazen I was to get you to notice me." She giggled when his eyes grew wide and his mouth gaped open.

"Brazen? You were so shy and naive.... That's why I've wondered all these years."

She tilted her head, cupped her fist and cuffed him on the chin. "You never suspected a thing did you, lover boy?"

"You little conniver, you. Here I thought all the while that I was bringing too much pressure on you to get into my bed. Woman, the mystery about you keeps getting deeper and deeper."

"You men always come up with that old cliché. There's no deep mystery. It's just that men are like that thin layer of ice on a small puddle, and we women just love to be the first to step on it. The cracking has such a lovely sound."

"You mean, we're that shallow?"

"No. 'Shallow' isn't the word for it. It's because you men, like the ice, are so transparent that we can see right through you. You think I don't

172

know that you pretend to be asleep in the morning when you give with that little squint. I'm wise to you, letting me be the first one out of bed so I can get things started, just so you can have your breakfast to order."

"Now, wait a minute. Do you really think I'm the kind of a man who would pretend to be asleep and wait for you to get up to fix my breakfast? How could you think such a thing?"

"You're so obvious in what you want, need and expect. You tip me off. I know exactly how you will react when you get what you set out to get. But to be fair, once I decided to go with you, I never hesitated, because for me, being with you was the most natural thing."

"I've always felt that way too. But since you sort of bared your soul, so to speak, and used me to chastise the whole male population, I'm going to tell you my secret. I've been carrying it around all these years." His voice trailed off and he grew silent again.

"Is it buried that deep, that I have to wait while you resurrect it from a subterranean passage in your brain?"

"Don't rush me. I really don't know how to say what I want to convey. Promise you won't laugh?"

"I promise."

"I was afraid I loved you more than I could prove. I was afraid that you would leave me when you discovered how inexperienced I was."

"Our love was as youthful as we were."

"I was so scared, I thought you'd see through the macho veneer I was trying to maintain. For sure, you'd think of ways to postpone it or call it off."

"Call it off? After I worked so hard to get where you wanted me?"

"You're teasing me. I can tell. Although I still can't believe you wanted me, or more than that, that you loved me. Really, do love me, even today?"

"Can't you tell how much you have enriched my life? I only want to know that I have done the same for you."

"You have, and more. But at last it has come out that you chased after me. You knew I would be your lover way before I even knew who you were? What is that? By all the rules and regulations, I'm the one who was supposed to have the ulterior motive of seducing you, and it turns out the other way around. It must be true, that women were made from Adam's rib."

"What do you mean by that?"

"I mean—well, let's put it this way. You know that old saying, 'Who knows what skullduggery lurks in the minds of men'?"

"That's not how it goes. Anyway, I still don't get the connection."

"I think you, my darling, along with your sisters, took away more than the rib. You grabbed some of that skullduggery that was given out to us, the chosen sex."

"The chosen sex? Don't make me laugh. If man did come first, it was only a test model, equipped with all the mistakes intact. The new and

improved model of choice was named... 'Woman.'
You old boys assume you have this great big wide
world of ours dangling at the end of your own
private yo-yo. Little do you realize that we women
allow you to dangle that yo-yo just so far before we
yank the cord."

"No, no, no. When I was a young man, you
used your womanly wiles on me to get me into bed,
and now that I'm older, you want to play hard to
get." He rolled over to take her in his arms and let
her hands gently trace the frame of his body as he
pressed himself firmly against her. His lips brushed
her eyelids before they found hers.

She knew he loved her, totally and
completely. And she was secure in his love. She
broke the silence of their lovely, Maxfield Parrish
morning.

"I consent," she said, "and I'll get up and
make your breakfast."

"Well, that all depends on what you're going
to serve me."

"How about some poached eggs, Mister
Lucky?"

***